THE GUNSMITH GIANT

A GUNSMITH TURKEY SHOOT

A Giant Holiday Gunsmith Adventure

**Books by J.R. Roberts
(Robert J. Randisi)**

Gunsmith Giant series

The Gunsmith series

Lady Gunsmith series

Angel Eyes series

Tracker series

Mountain Jack Pike series

COMING SOON!
The Gunsmith
480 – The Friendly Gold Mine

For more information visit:
www.SpeakingVolumes.us

THE GUNSMITH GIANT

A GUNSMITH TURKEY SHOOT

A Giant Holiday Gunsmith Adventure

J.R. Roberts

SPEAKING VOLUMES, LLC
NAPLES, FLORIDA
2022

A Gunsmith Turkey Shoot

ISBN 978-1-64540-867-3

Chapter One

With all the major accomplishments in Abraham Lincoln's life, one thing that people would probably overlook was his naming, in 1863, Thanksgiving as a major holiday.

Clint Adams knew Lincoln, as he had served in the Union Army as an agent for E.J. Allan, an alias used during his wartime service by Alan Pinkerton. Although a very young man, Clint was sometimes known as "The President's Man."

After Lincoln's assassination, Clint chose not to re-enlist in the Union Army, and also refused to work for Pinkerton in his detective agency. Although he had worked for subsequent presidents since that time, he only thought fondly of President Abraham Lincoln, especially during the Thanksgiving season.

Clint received many invitations from friends across the country to share Thanksgiving dinner, but for the most part he spent his Thanksgivings alone under the stars, his only company his horse. In the beginning it was his big black gelding, Duke, followed by his Darley Arabian, Eclipse, and now his Tobiano, Toby.

However, this year he was considering accepting one of his invitations. For some reason he wasn't looking forward to spending this Thanksgiving alone, with his only companion the Tobiano.

He was still thinking about which invitation to accept as he rode into Belle Fourche. It wasn't far from Deadwood, but since his friend Wild Bill Hickok was killed there, he avoided it.

Considering he was already in Belle Fourche, and still heading north, it seemed likely he would accept the invitation to spend Thanksgiving with his friend Bull Sturdivant and his family.

But Sturdivant's home was still several days away, and there was time for Clint to change his mind. After all, the Sturdivants had several children. Although it might be fun to hunt some wild turkey and see the looks on their faces when he brought one home for the whole family. But they might be big enough now that one bird wasn't enough.

It had been some time since he had seen Belle Fourche, and during that time the town had grown some. He remembered there being one saloon in town, but now he rode down the town's main street and saw four of them, three looking newly erected.

It didn't matter to Clint which hotel he stayed in, since he only intended to spend one night in town, so he reined in his Tobiano in front of the Belle House and went in to register. When he had his key, he went back out and walked the Tobiano to the nearest livery stable. Once he was sure his horse was in good hands, he took his rifle and saddlebags and walked back to the hotel.

The room was large and clean with a comfortable bed, an armchair, a chest of drawers with a pitcher and basin on it. He put his rifle in a corner and the saddlebags on the armchair. He hadn't been in the room five minutes when there was a knock at the door.

"Who is it?" he asked.

"Sheriff Haley," a man's voice said. "I'd like to talk to you, Mr. Adams."

Clint still had his gunbelt on, so he went to the door and opened it. A tall, rangy man wearing a badge stood there and actually took a step back when Clint appeared.

"What can I do for you, Sheriff?" Clint asked.

"As soon as the desk clerk saw your name, he came to my office to tell me you were here."

"Is there some reason why I shouldn't be here?" Clint asked.

"No, no, not at all," the sheriff said. "I don't know if you saw the signs as you rode in, but we're havin' a turkey shoot so some folks can win a turkey for Thanksgiving. You see, a lot of folks in town can't afford to buy one."

"So how much are you charging them to take part in the shoot?"

"That's just it, sir," the lawman said, "we're not charging 'em anything. We just want to give some folks an opportunity to win themselves a turkey for the holiday."

"And what's that got you do with me?" Clint asked.

"Well, I was just hopin' you weren't intendin' to take part in the shoot," the sheriff said. "You see, I'm pretty sure there ain't a marksman in town who could beat the Gunsmith."

"You don't have anything to worry about, Sheriff," Clint said. "I didn't know anything about this shoot, and now that I do, I don't intend to compete."

"Well," the lawman said, "that's just fine, then. I hope you enjoy your stay in our town."

"I'm just going to be here long enough for a meal, and a night in a real bed, and then I'll be moving on."

"Let's just be clear," the lawman said, "I'm not tellin' you to leave town."

"I get it, Sheriff," Clint said. "You just don't want me to win the turkey shoot."

"Exactly."

"Don't worry, then," Clint said. "I won't even enter."

"Then thanks for your time," the sheriff said. "Enjoy your stay."

The lawman left, and Clint wondered what that was all about.

Chapter Two

After the lawman left the room, Clint decided to go down to the street and find someplace to have a meal. Maybe, along the way, he would find out something about this turkey shoot.

In the lobby, instead of looking for a restaurant, he decided to ask the clerk.

"Where can I get a decent meal?"

"Oh, uh, there's a small café just down the street that does a good stew, or steak," the young man said, nervously.

"Thanks," Clint said. "Do you always let the sheriff know when strangers come to town?"

"Uh, well, no," the clerk said

"So you recognized my name and thought you should tell him?"

"Um, yes sir."

"Well, I tell you what," Clint said. "I'd appreciate it if you didn't tell anyone else I was here."

"Um, yes sir—I mean, no sir."

"If the word gets around, I'll know where to look for the source."

"B-but—the sheriff knows, too. He might tell some-one."

"That's right, he might," Clint said. "The café, do I make a left out the door, or a right?"

"Oh, a left," the man said.

"Then I must've passed it on the way to the livery."

"It's a small place," the clerk said. "You could uh, miss it if you're not lookin'."

"Then I'll look," Clint said. "Thanks."

"Oh, uh, yessir."

Clint went out the door and turned left. Within a block he came to a tiny café. The clerk was right, he would have missed it if he wasn't looking.

Although Belle Fourche had grown since he was last through there, the street was still kind of empty for that time of day.

"A table, sir?" an older man wearing a white apron asked as he entered.

"Yes, thank you," Clint said.

"As you can see, you can take your pick." Each of the ten tables were presently empty.

"I'll take one in the back," Clint said. He walked to a rear table, removed his fur-lined jacket, hung it on the back of the chair, and sat. "The clerk at the hotel said you make a good stew."

"We do, sir," the man said. "An excellent stew."

Clint had been thinking of a steak, but the cold of South Dakota made him change his mind.

"I'll have the stew."

"Right away, sir."

"And coffee."

"Yes, sir."

The coffee came first, and Clint sipped it while he waited for the stew. When it came, the waiter carried the steaming bowl with a towel.

"I've also got a basket of biscuits for you," he said.

"Sounds good," Clint said.

"Be careful with that," the man said, setting the bowl down, "it's hot."

The waiter hurried to the kitchen and returned with a basket of warm biscuits.

"Can I get you anythin' else, sir?" he asked.

"No, this is fine. You could answer some questions, though."

"Yes, sir?"

"Is it always this empty at this time of day?" Clint asked.

"Most of the citizens are at the other end of town."

"What are they doing there?" Clint asked.

"Signing up for the turkey shoot."

"Oh yes, I heard something about that," Clint said. "When is it supposed to take place?"

"The day before Thanksgiving."

"Is the whole town entering to win one turkey?" Clint asked.

"Oh no, sir," the man said. "There'll be ten turkeys up for grabs."

"Ten?" Clint asked. "There are that many wild turkeys around here?"

"Oh, yes sir," the waiter said. "They've been seen close by. No one knows why, but they're not as scarce as they once were."

Clint figured the stew had probably cooled a bit, so he tried a spoonful.

"This is very good," Clint said.

"If you'd rather have a fork—" the clerk started, but Clint cut him off.

"No," he said, "this is going to be fine."

"Then if you'll excuse me, there should be some more customers, soon. I've got to get ready for them."

"That's okay," Clint said. "I don't want to hold you up."

The waiter returned to the kitchen and Clint turned all his attention to the tasty stew and flaky biscuits.

Chapter Three

Clint continued to enjoy his meal as townspeople began to enter. Before long the little café had every table full. Not many of the people paid any attention to the stranger, and most of the conversations seemed to be about the coming turkey shoot.

At a couple of tables wives were warning their husbands that they better come home with a turkey. At another two men were bragging to each other about how many turkeys they would win. At another a man was assuring his wife and two daughters that he would come home with a big turkey.

Clint noticed a woman enter and sit alone. She was in her thirties, red-haired and attractive. He watched as she crossed the room, sat at a table close to him and ordered the stew. She didn't seem to be paying any attention to anyone else in the room.

Clint had almost finished his meal when the woman leaned over and said to him, "These people all seem so sure of themselves. If there were that many turkeys out there, the town would be overrun with them."

"Are you not entering the turkey shoot?" he asked.

"I wasn't going to," she confided, "but seeing all of these people who are, I just might."

"You've no confidence in them?"

She smiled.

"I know most of these people," she said. "There's not a marksman among them. I don't think any of them can hit the side of a barn."

"And you can?"

"Well," she said, "I can hit a turkey. Do you mind if I join you? Instead of talking this way?"

"Please do," he said.

She picked up her bowl and drink and carried them to his table.

"Oh, you're almost finished," she said. "I've only just got mine."

"I'm still going to clean my bowl with some biscuits," he assured her.

"Ah," she said, getting to her feet, "I left my biscuits." She retrieved the basket from her table and rejoined him. "Now we have plenty. My name is Letitia Miller."

"Letitia," he said. "That's a pretty name."

"Most folks around here call me Letty."

"Letty it is, then," Clint said. "My name's Clint."

"No last name?"

"Adams," he said. "It's Adams."

"It's a pleasure to meet you, Mr. Adams."

"Please, call me Clint."

"What brings you to Belle Fourche, Clint?" she asked. "Certainly not the turkey shoot."

"No," he said, "I didn't know anything about it when I checked into the hotel."

"Well, you know about it now," she said. "Might you be interested?"

"Not at all," he said. "In fact, I was invited not to compete."

"By who?"

"The sheriff."

"Are you serious?" she asked. Then she looked like something just occurred to her. "Oh, wait. Adams."

Clint nodded.

"That's why he invited you not to shoot," she said. "You're that Clint Adams."

"Right."

"Who told him you were in town?"

"The desk clerk."

"Which hotel?"

"The Belle House," he told her.

"Oh, that's Lenny," she said. "Lots of folks call him Lenny Loud Mouth."

"So he's going to tell everyone I'm here?"

"He probably already has," she said.

Clint sighed and shook his head. "I guess I'll have to leave town."

"Why?"

"Usually when folks hear I'm in town, it gives somebody the idea to take a shot at me."

"Not in this town," she told him.

"Why not?"

"These folks are pacifists."

"Well, I should still leave . . ."

"When?" she asked.

"Probably in the morning," he said.

"Did you intend to stay longer?"

"Well, I was on my way to join a friend and his family for the holiday, but I thought it might be fun to see this turkey shoot," he said. "What's it going to be like?"

"There's two parts," she said.

"What are they?"

"A wild turkey hunt," she said. "You can go out and shoot your own."

"Or?"

"Or you shoot at targets, and the winner gets a great, big, wild turkey."

"Which one would you do?"

"I'm a hunter," she said. "I can shoot targets but hunting them gives them a fair chance."

"That's true."

"But I won't be competing."

What's all this excitement about wild turkeys?"

"You haven't heard?" she asked. "They've been scarce around here for years. Now, all of a sudden, they're back."

"And people are anxious to shoot them," he commented.

"Right," she said. "Especially since Thanksgiving is coming."

"Well," he said, "I guess it could be entertaining to watch."

"So you might stay past tomorrow?"

"I might, as long as nobody tries to take a shot at me instead of a turkey."

"When do you think you'll make up your mind?"

"Probably in the morning."

"That works out fine for me," she said.

"In what way?"

"It gives me all night to convince you to stay a while." The look on her lovely face made her meaning clear.

He smiled.

"And how do you plan to do that?"

She smiled back.

"How do you think?"

Chapter Four

Clint waited while Letty finished her meal, during which he drank some more coffee while they talked. They didn't discuss her intention to convince him to stay in town, or how she planned to do it, but when she finished eating and he paid the check they left and went right to his hotel room.

When he closed the door he turned and asked her, "Aren't you afraid of what Lenny Loud Mouth will say?"

"Not at all," she said, undoing the belt on her trousers.

He had walked to the hotel slightly behind her, enjoying the way her hips swayed and her body moved in her trousers.

Now he watched with great interest as she undressed. She did it with very little feminine flair. Rather, she was in a great hurry to get her boots and clothes off. And while he still didn't know what she did for a living, it obviously didn't require feminine underthings. So, in moments she was naked, standing there without posing or posturing, the way many women did. Instead, she put her hands on her hips, looked at him and said, "Well?"

"Oh," he said, "sorry. I was . . . watching."

"Well, now I want to watch." She took her hands off her wide hips and folded her arms beneath her full, solid breasts.

"O-kay," he said. He removed his gunbelt, put it aside

Within easy reach, pulled off his boots and trousers. That left only his shirt to remove, but as he unbuttoned it, she came forward, reached out and grabbed hold of him.

"Come here, you," she said, tugging him to the bed.

He went quite willingly, and as she climbed onto the bed he whipped off his shirt and joined her. She was a solidly built, strong woman who wasn't afraid to show what she wanted and went after it.

She pushed him down onto his back, straddled him and kissed him, roughly, deeply and, to his utter delight, wetly. It was as if she wanted to devour him, and he didn't mind in the least. He returned the kiss with equal fervor. He tried to put his arms around her and hold her there, but that wasn't what she wanted at that moment. She broke his grip, shimmied down his body and drove her face into his crotch with avid lips and tongue. She wet the length of him fully, and then took him into her mouth and began to suck. Still unaware of what she did for a living, he doubted she was a whore, but she certainly knew what she was doing in bed. He allowed her to enjoy him for as long as he could take it, and then decided to match her strength for strength. He reached down and pulled himself free of her mouth, then tugged her up onto her back and proceeded to explore her body with his hands, tongue and lips.

All her strength drained from her as she gave herself up to the pleasure he was giving her.

"My God," she gasped, "I've never had a man do this to me before."

"That's a shame," he said. "You should experience this all the time."

"I've always thought men were too selfish for this," she told him.

"Maybe the men you've met have been," he said, stroking her with his fingertips. "We're not all like that."

"You're the only one I've met so far," she said, "who isn't."

"Well then," Clint said, "just relax and enjoy."

And she did. She enjoyed his fingertips on her skin, his lips on her inner thighs, and finally his tongue delving into her, and swooping over her, bringing wave after wave of pleasure until she was gasping for air . . .

***

She snuggled up against him later and asked, "Do you do this to all your women?"

"All my women?"

"I assume a man who treats women this way has many," she said. "Is there a wife? A girlfriend?"

"No," he said, "no one."

"But you've had many women."

"I've been with a lot of women, yes," he said. "I wouldn't say I've had many. That makes it sound like I owned them."

"Believe me," she said, sliding her hand down his chest, "a man who can do what you do can own any woman he wants."

"I don't want to own anyone," he said. "When I'm with a woman I just want to make her glad she's with me."

"Oh, you've done that tonight already," she said, moving her hand lower so she could stroke him, "and we're not done."

"We're not?"

She closed her hand over him, laughed and said, "Not by a long shot."

She continued to stroke him until he was fully hard again, then leaned down and took him in her mouth again. This time he let her suck him as long as she wanted, and she didn't stop until he swelled and exploded with a loud, long, guttural groan . . .

***

She was serious about not being done, because in the morning he woke with her on him again. This time she had straddled him while he was still asleep, and he woke with her riding him until he exploded once again . . .

Chapter Five

They laid together with the morning sunlight coming in the window and covering them.

"Can I convince you to stay for the shoot?" she asked.

"Thanksgiving is still days away," he said.

"Do you have somewhere else to go?"

"Yes, and no."

"What's that mean?"

"It means I have invitations, but I haven't accepted one, yet."

"Then accept mine," she said, snuggling up to him. "Stay with me until after Thanksgiving."

He looked down at her strong, solid body pressed up against his.

"Well?"

"Let's just say that, right now, your invitation tops my list."

"That's good," she said. "I'll have to keep working on you."

"I don't think I'd object to that," he said. "Can we start with breakfast?"

"You've had enough of me?" She grabbed hold of him in her powerful grip.

"You've worked up my appetite," he said. "I'll need sustenance to keep on going."

She released her hold on him and said, "Then by all means, let's go to breakfast."

***

They went back to the small café where they had met and sat at the same table.

"Had you seen me before you came in here yesterday?" he asked.

"Never," she said. "When I walked in, it was the first time. But I knew I wanted to be with you."

"It seemed to me like you never noticed me."

"Oh, I noticed you," she said. "I just kept it to myself until I was seated."

He noticed, while they ate, that other diners in the place were watching them.

"Do all these people know you?" he asked.

"They do."

"Yesterday they didn't seem to."

"They know better than to bother me during a meal," she said.

"Whatever business you're in must affect them all," he said.

"It does," she said.

"Then I guess I should ask you what business you're in?" he asked.

She smiled.

"Politics."

"Politics?"

She nodded.

"I'm the Mayor of Belle Fourche."

His eyebrows went up.

"I'm impressed," he said. "I've never met a female mayor, before."

"I fell into the job," she said. "Nobody else wanted it, and the town needed someone to take charge."

"And you don't mind everyone knowing—or thinking they know—what we were doing all night?"

"I may be mayor, but I'm also a woman," she said. "I need to eat, drink, and fuck. And it's been a long time since I did the last one."

"Why's that?"

"I told you," she said. "All the men I know and have known are selfish bastards. You've given me hope. But I'm afraid, when you finally leave, I'm going to continue to be disappointed."

"You'll give somebody a chance," he said. "Maybe they'll change your mind."

"There aren't too many Clint Adams' in this world."

He laughed.

"Let's hope."

***

After breakfast they left the café and she said, "I'm afraid I have to go home, take a bath, and dress for work."

"I'm sure you're a very busy woman," he said.

"Especially today," she said. "There's a meeting of the town council."

"About serious matters, I'm sure."

"Oh yes," she said, "the turkey shoot."

"That doesn't sound so serious."

"You'd be surprised."

"I'll let you get to it then."

She placed her hand on his chest.

"Come by City Hall later and we'll have dinner," she said. "I'll tell you all about it."

"I'll be there, Miss Mayor," he promised. "I'll be there."

Chapter Six

Left to his own devices, Clint decided to take a closer look at Belle Fourche and see what had resulted from its growing pains.

Although it had been years, the town seemed to have grown by two-thirds. He wondered why no one had wanted the mayor's job, leaving it to Letty Miller to snatch up.

In addition to three more hotels, Belle Fourche had six saloons that Clint could see and probably more on some of the side streets. And it had much larger restaurants than the café he had already eaten in. He wondered how the food was in some of them, thought he would probably find out when dining with the mayor?

Once he realized the town was too big to walk through in one day, he decided to check out a saloon or two.

He found one called The South of Deadwood Saloon. Seemed being located south of Deadwood was good enough reason for its name.

The saloon was doing a good business. He figured the later the day got, the better it would get. He went to the bar and elbowed himself some room.

"Beer," he told the bored looking barkeep.

The man nodded and set a cold mug in front of him.

"Who owns this place?" he asked.

"Mr. Kittredge."

"Where is he?"

"In his office," the bartender said, "back of the room."

"Any security here?"

Suddenly, the bartender didn't look so bored.

"Two," he said, "front and back,"

"Tell them to take it easy," Clint said. "I'm not looking for trouble."

The bartender nodded, then turned and waved to two men.

"Thanks."

Clint picked up his beer and walked to the back of the room. He drew stares along the way, but that didn't bother him. When he reached the door, he knocked.

"Come in!" a man's deep voice called.

He opened the door and stepped through. A man seated behind a desk looked at him. He appeared to be in his forties, was wearing a shirt with long sleeves. A jacket hung on the back of his chair.

"Can I help you, friend?"

"Are you Kittredge?"

"I'm Arthur Kittredge."

"My name's Clint Adams."

"I heard you were in town."

"I figured word would get around."

"Come on in and have a seat," Kittredge invited. "Tell me what's on your mind."

Clint sat across from him in a comfortable chair.

"You happy with that beer or can I offer you some good whiskey?"

"This'll do."

"Then what can I do for you?"

"I'm curious about this town's mayor."

"Letty Miller? What about her?"

"Is she serious?"

"About runnin' this town? Dead serious."

"She told me she only got the job because nobody else wanted it."

"That's partially true."

"What do you mean?"

"I mean nobody else wanted it because they knew she did."

"Does she scare people?"

"She scares everybody," Kittredge said.

"Including you?"

"I just want to run my saloon," Kittredge said. "She can have the town."

"And this turkey shoot?" Clint asked. "It's on the level?"

"The turkeys are back this year, for some reason, and it's the mayor's idea. Without it a lot of people wouldn't have turkey for Thanksgiving, so yeah, it's on the level. Why?" Kittredge asked. "Are you interested? I don't see anybody else having a chance if you are."

"No, no," Clint said, "I was just curious and thought a saloon owner and businessman would know the details."

"Well, that's it," Kittredge said. "Tell me, have you met the mayor?"

"I have, although she didn't tell me right away who she was."

"Is she tryin' to get you involved?"

"To tell you the truth, I don't know what her end game is," Clint said. "Are you on the town council?"

"Not me," Kittredge said. "I have no interest in politics."

"Well," Clint said, "thanks for your time."

"I'll walk you out," Kittredge said.

The two men left the office and walked to the front door under the watchful gaze of most of the customers.

"Any idea how long you'll be in town?" Kittredge asked. "I can put together a poker game, if you're interested."

"I don't know my plans," Clint said, "but I'll let you know."

"Come back in any time," Kittredge said at the door.

The two men shook hands, and Clint left.

***

After Clint left the saloon, a man stood up from a table and walked over to Kittredge.

"What was that about?" he asked.

"To tell you the truth, I don't rightly know."

"That was Clint Adams, wasn't it? The Gunsmith?"

"It sure was."

"What'd he want?"

"He just had some questions about the mayor and the turkey shoot."

"Is he enterin'?"

"He says no."

"He can't be here for no reason," the man said.

"Keep an eye on him, Trevor," Kittredge said, "but don't get too close."

"Right."

"He might have some connection to the mayor. Keep that in mind."

"That bitch!"

"Just settle down and watch," Kittredge said, "That's all I want you to do."

"Sure, boss," Trevor said, and went out the door.

Chapter Seven

Clint left the South of Deadwood Saloon, surprised that the man had spoken so freely to him. It was almost as if Kittredge had been expecting him. He wondered just how far word had spread that he was in town. Lenny Loud Mouth had apparently been very busy.

Of course, Letty's interest in him could have just been the sex. It had happened to him before with women. But why had Kittredge been so willing to talk? The man certainly didn't appear to be intimidated.

He spotted the man following him almost as soon as he left the saloon. It figured that Kittredge had put the man on his tail, probably to see what Clint's plans might be. If that was the case, the man could be following him for a long time, because Clint didn't even know what his plans were.

Sex with Letty Miller was certainly worth a few more days in Belle Fourche. But she seemed like an intelligent woman and if the thought wasn't there before, it had probably occurred to her now that he could be helpful to her. The best thing to do would probably be just to ask her, and he could do that over dinner.

As far as the man Kittredge had put on his tail, he didn't sense any impending danger. If the saloon owner just wanted him followed out of curiosity, no harm done. In fact, Clint decided to let the man follow him all day. That included when he went to dinner with the mayor. Let Kittredge wonder what that was all about.

Clint went to his hotel room and spent the afternoon cleaning his guns. A couple of looks out the window told him his tail was still there, across the street from the hotel. With a smile on his face, he decided to take a nap . . .

***

When he woke, the man was still there. He freshened up using the pitcher-and-basin in the room, then strapped on his gunbelt, put on his hat and left the room.

It was his intention to walk to City Hall to meet up with the mayor for supper. There was no harm in allowing the man to follow him there, but he had an amusing thought.

He started toward City Hall, which he had located during his walk around town. After turning a corner, he stepped into a doorway and waited. When his tail appeared, he stepped out and blocked the man's path. The man stopped short and gaped at him in surprise. He was young, probably in his twenties, and while he obviously knew how to do what he was told, he seemed a bit confused by the change in the situation.

"Wha—"

"I understand it's your job to tail me," Clint said, "so you might as well know I'm on my way to City Hall to have dinner with the mayor."

"Whataya—"

"I thought this would give you time to report back to Kittredge, and maybe get some food yourself."

"I dunno—"

"I don't have more time to spend with you," Clint said, "so I guess I'll see you later."

He turned and walked away, leaving the young man looking both dismayed and confused. When he regained his senses, he turned and headed for The South of Deadwood Saloon to see how his boss would take this news, and what he would want him to do.

***

When Clint arrived at City Hall, he expected to have to go to the mayor's office to announce his presence. Instead, he found her waiting outside for him.

"Right on time," she said. "I thought I'd take you to one of the bigger, better restaurants in town."

"I'm in your hands," he told her.

"Not yet," she said, smiling, "but you will be."

Chapter Eight

Mayor Miller took Clint to a rather large restaurant called The Chop House. The waiter walked them across the crowded room to what was obviously Letty's regular table. Along the way she exchanged some greetings with her constituents, but when they were seated, they were suddenly ignored.

"I'm curious," Clint said, "why didn't you tell me you were the mayor right away?"

"I didn't want to be the mayor when I was with you," she answered, "I just wanted to be Letty."

"Well," he said, "you certainly were that."

As the waiter, an older, white-haired man, came back to take their order she said, "You'll want a steak here."

"I'll leave it to you."

"Two steak dinners, William," she said to the waiter.

"Yes, Miss Mayor."

"Seems like today you're the mayor," Clint said.

"I accepted the job, so most days I have to do it," she pointed out.

"I heard around town that you rule with an iron fist."

"You heard that around town?" she asked. "I'll bet you heard that from one of the business owners. In fact, I'll bet it was a saloon owner."

"You got that right, it was."

"Which one?" she asked, then quickly blurted, "Wait, don't tell me. I'll bet a man like you was curious, so you went into The South of Deadwood Saloon. That would make it Mr. Kittredge."

"I don't want to get anyone in trouble," he said.

"Ah ha, it was Kittredge!" she said, triumphantly.

Clint picked up his glass of water and drank from it.

"All right, don't tell me," she said. "I like a man who can keep his mouth shut at the right time."

"What about that iron hand?"

"Would that bother you, if it was true?" she asked. "I wouldn't have thought you were the kind of man who felt threatened by a strong woman."

"Oh, I'm not," he said. "I thought I proved that last night."

The waiter returned with two platters laden with meat and vegetables. He also set down a basket of hot, flakey biscuits.

"Anything else, Miss?"

"No, thank you, William."

While buttering a biscuit Clint said, "I would've thought he'd call you Madame Mayor."

"He did when I first got into office, but I told him I preferred 'Miss.' 'Madame' brings something else to mind."

"I understand."

They cut into their steaks and began eating. Clint found the meat perfect.

"So tell me, Miss Mayor," he said, "how did your Town Council meeting go?"

"Don't even ask," she said. "They're a bunch of men with a female mayor. They were not happy with some of my plans for the town."

"Like the turkey shoot?"

"Exactly," she said. "They don't understand what having a happy population at Thanksgiving can mean to a town."

"I guess they're going to find out," Clint said.

"You bet they are," she said, "but I don't want to talk about that. What'd you do today?"

"I took a look at your town," he said. "It's grown since I was last this way."

"And it's going to grow more. Did you talk with some of the townspeople?"

"I did."

"And what was the consensus?"

"Seems like quite a few people are afraid of you."

"Well, that's their problem," she said. "Who did you hear that from, Kittredge?"

"He did have some pretty strong opinions," Clint said. "Why isn't the owner of the biggest saloon in town on the Town Council?"

"First," she said, "they don't want him there, and second, he doesn't want to be there."

Clint figured that was actually second and third. He figured first was, Letty didn't want him there.

"And to tell you the truth," she said, as if she knew what he was thinking, "I don't much want him there, either. He's got some ideas of his own that don't match mine."

"I got that feeling," Clint said. "He also put a man on my trail."

"That doesn't surprise me," she said. "He's going to think I brought you here for some reason. Or that I'm keeping you here for one."

"That second is probably true," he said.

She laughed.

"You know it."

"I couldn't help noticing as I walked around how empty the town was."

"That's because most of the people were at the south end, signing up for the shoot."

"It sounds like you're going to have a couple of successful events."

"And I want the success to go much further than that," she said, and went back to her steak.

Chapter Nine

Over coffee and pie, Clint made a decision. He wanted everything to be out in the open, and on the up-and-up.

"Letty, let's put all our cards on the table."

Apparently, she had made the same decision.

"All right," she said, "everything on the up-and-up. I slept with you last night because I wanted to. I needed a man, and as the mayor, I couldn't very well just choose a local. When I saw you in the café, I knew you were the right one."

"And you didn't know who I was?"

"No, not at first," she said. "Not until you introduced yourself."

"And then?"

"Oh, I still wanted to sleep with you," she said, "and that turned out to be a very good decision. But afterward . . . well . . ."

"You decided you could use me."

"Clint—"

"No, it's okay," he said. "Just tell me what's on your mind."

"You're right, it's the turkey shoot," she said. "I need someone to be in charge and run it. And having the Gunsmith would make it an even bigger event."

"So you don't want me to take part in it."

"No," she said, "the sheriff was right about that. I just need someone to . . . to spearhead it."

Clint studied the woman, wondering if he could look past his natural distrust of politicians and take her at her word.

"I understand your reluctance," she said. "Politicians are a dishonest bunch. I just hope you'll find it in your heart to believe that I just want to do something good for my town."

"I'm going to need more information," Clint finally said. "I understand this contest is to be held in two parts?"

"The sheriff was supposed to officiate, but I'm sure he'll step down if you agree to do it. Why don't you talk it over with him?"

"I will," Clint said, "as long as you make it clear to him that it wasn't my idea."

"I will certainly tell him this was my idea," she said, "and I'll leave it to him whether to step down or not. I won't make it an order. We can go and talk to him now."

Clint lifted his coffee cup, drained it, set it down and said, "Let's go."

***

Clint accompanied Letty Miller to the office of Sheriff Haley. When they entered, the lawman jumped up from his chair.

"Miss Mayor," he said.

"Sheriff," Letty said. "Stay in your chair. Mr. Adams and I came to chat."

Haley eyed Clint warily as he retook his seat.

"About what?" he asked.

"The turkey shoot," she said. "Do you mind if we sit?"

Haley looked at Letty as if she was crazy for asking and said, "Uh, sure, go ahead."

Clint could see the man was wondering how they got together about the turkey shoot.

When they were both seated Letty said, "I've proposed to Mr. Adams that he run the shoot, Sheriff."

"*You* proposed it?" the lawman said.

"That's right."

"But I'm supposed to run it."

"I think you can see how much bigger an event it would be if the Gunsmith ran it, can't you?"

"Well, yeah, I guess . . ."

"So you wouldn't have any objection to stepping down," she said.

She said it in the form of a question, but it sounded to Clint like an order.

"I have a better idea," Clint said to her.

"Oh? What's that?"

"Why don't the sheriff and I run it together?" Clint suggested.

"Then if he agrees to that you'd do it?" she asked him.

"You said the contest takes place the day before Thanksgiving?"

"Yes," she said, "but we would be glad to give you a wonderful Thanksgiving dinner the next day. In fact, I'll cook it myself."

"You'll cook it?" the lawman asked, obviously surprised.

Letty looked at him.

"What's wrong? Don't you think I can cook?"

"Oh, sure," the lawman said, "if you say you can cook, you can cook."

"Then it's settled," she said. "You and Clint Adams will co-officiate the turkey shoot." She stood up. "I'll leave you two to make plans." She turned to Clint. "I'll see you later, Clint." She looked at Haley. "Sheriff."

"Miss Mayor."

She left the office.

"I didn't know you and the mayor knew each other," Haley said.

"We didn't," Clint said, "until yesterday. Shall we get started?"

Chapter Ten

Briefly, Sheriff Haley went over the rules of the contest with Clint. While the man talked, Clint wondered how he had gotten himself mixed up in something like this?

"On the first day, two days before Thanksgiving, we go hunting and folks get to shoot their own turkeys. But the shot has to be in the neck so as not to damage the main part of the bird."

"And what about the birds that *are* damaged?" Clint asked.

"They'll be cleaned overnight, and then the winners on the second day each get a turkey."

"And the second day is target shooting?"

"That's right."

"And whose idea was this two-day event?" Clint asked.

"The mayor wanted it to last two days," the lawman said. "I came up with the rules."

"And you're the judge?"

"I was," Haley said. "Now it's the two of us."

"And people are signing up now?"

"Yesterday was the first day," Haley said, "and today is the second. We had plenty of 'em. Tomorrow we post the names of the competitors, and the times they begin their shoots."

"Okay, the names are posted on Monday. First day of shooting is Tuesday and the second on Wednesday."

"Right."

"Where's the list of sign-ups?"

Haley opened his desk drawer and took out a sheaf of papers.

"Right here," he said, slapping them down. "We need to work out the times, and how many people shoot at what times."

"Tonight?"

"We can start in the mornin'," Haley said.

"Okay," Clint asked, "what time do you want me here?"

"After breakfast," Haley said. "Say . . . nine?"

"Nine a.m. it is."

Clint stood and headed for the door.

"Adams?"

Clint turned and looked at the man.

"Why're you doin' this?"

Clint shrugged and said, "I've got nothing better to do."

He left the office.

***

Arthur Kittredge went to the second floor of the South of Deadwood Saloon and entered his room. The naked woman in his bed was a vision of loveliness and sex.

"Don't worry," she assured him, "no one saw me come up here."

She got to her knees on the bed, and, in that position, her proud breasts were thrust out at him. They were round and solid, tipped with large, pink nipples.

"Is it done?" he asked.

"It's done."

"He agreed?"

"He did."

Kittredge removed his jacket and tossed it on a chair, followed it with his shirt. Then sat in the chair to remove his shoes. That done, he stood and pulled off his pants. That left him standing there in his underwear. Although forty-eight, he was a man who kept himself in good condition.

The woman left the bed, crossed the room to him and got on her knees. She tugged his shorts down, and a long, semi-erect penis just about leaped out at her.

She took hold of his cock and stroked it.

"I guess you had to go all out to convince him, huh?" he asked, looking down at her.

She glanced up at him while stroking him.

"Not quite all out," she said. "I generally save that for you."

He reached down and pulled her to her feet in front of him and gathered her into his arms. The heat from both their naked bodies was intense.

"You're going to have to prove that to me," he told her.

Chapter Eleven

Clint had been in bed for an hour when a knock came at the door.

"Sorry I'm late," the mayor said, as he let her in. She quickly began to remove her clothes. "Business."

When she was naked, she removed Clint's underwear and tugged him toward the bed.

"How did you and the sheriff get along?" she asked, pressing him down onto his back.

"Fine," he said. "We'll get started tomorrow, assigning start times to contestants."

She slid atop him, and he could feel her pussy was already wet. Lifting her hips, she slid down, taking him into her steamy, hot depths.

"Let's not talk for a little while," she said, closing her eyes. "I've needed this for most of the day."

He gave her the requested silence, and she simply rode up and down on him, slowly, seeking her release, but in no hurry to find it . . .

***

In the morning the woman dressed and asked Kittredge, "Are you gonna shoot?"

"I prefer to buy my turkeys," the saloon owner said. "Are you going to cook for your husband?"

"That sonofabitch can catch and cook his own bird," she snarled. She leaned over the bed and kissed Kittredge. "I'll see you later tonight, if you're not busy with Miss Mayor."

"Mayor Miller and I are business associates, that's all," he told her. "You know that."

"You know, and I know, but does she know that?"

She waved and flounced out the door.

Kittredge decided to sleep another hour before dressing and going downstairs.

***

Clint woke the next morning with Letty Miller lying heavily across his chest. He reached down and stroked the smooth skin of her shoulders and back. He ran one finger along the crack of her ass, and she stirred.

"More?" she asked. "I'm still tired from the last time."

"It's morning," he said. "I thought Miss Mayor might have to go to work."

She groaned and rolled onto her back.

"Why did I take this job?" she asked. "I'd so much rather stay here in bed with you until noon."

"Well now, I have to go to work, thanks to you," he said. "The sheriff is going to be waiting for me, and I'll need a full breakfast."

"Breakfast" she said, brightening. "That's a fine idea."

She sprang out of bed and grabbed her dress.

"I'll see you at the café."

"Why not walk there with me?"

"I have to go home, clean up, and dress," she said. "I can't be seen in the same clothes I was wearing yesterday. Besides, I smell!"

"You smell fine to me," he said.

"Fine for a roll in the hay," she said. "Not so fine to be around decent people."

She went to him and pressed his face between her solid breasts.

"Inhale, then," she said, "and carry my scent with you all day."

He breathed in deeply, and when he grabbed for her, she danced away and dressed.

"Later, my sweet man," she said at the door and rushed out.

***

After a quick breakfast with the lady mayor, Clint walked over to the sheriff's office.

"Just in time," Sheriff Haley said. His desk was covered with papers. "Let's get to it."

Clint sat across from the man and they got started.

Haley knew all there was to know about the competitors. He suggested early starts for some, late for others, and Clint simply went along with it. He knew he was just a figurehead to bring more attention to the contest, so he argued with none of the sheriff's decisions. Still, it took most of the morning and afternoon before they were done.

"I'll post these a few places in town, and we'll be ready to start tomorrow mornin'," Haley said.

"I'll walk around and post with you so folks see me," Clint said.

"Suit yerself."

The sheriff gathered up the sheets and they left the office to nail them up all over town.

"You got any deputies who can help you with this?" Clint asked.

"The town won't give me the money for deputies," Haley complained. "If you don't want to do this, I can do it alone."

"No, no," Clint said, "according to the mayor, we're in this together."

"Yeah," Sheriff Haley grumbled, "together."

Chapter Twelve

After posting all the notices, they went to the South of Deadwood Saloon for a beer.

"I haven't been to any of the other saloons in town, yet," Clint commented.

"No point," Haley said. "You're in the best one, right now."

They went to the crowded bar, elbowed themselves some room and ordered a beer each. The men they had nudged stared at them, and either recognized Clint or saw Haley's badge, and gave them even more room.

"You think you know who's going to win this thing?" Clint asked.

"We have some good hunters hereabouts," Haley said. "I think quite a few will get their birds tomorrow. But when they go on to target shootin', I don't know."

"You must have some idea who the marksmen in town are," Clint said.

"We've got quite a few," Haley admitted, "I just can't hazard a guess about who's gonna win. C'mon, let's get a table."

They grabbed their beers and walked across the floor to a table.

"Tell me about some of the people in town," Clint requested.

"Like who?"

"Let's start with Arthur Kittredge."

"A ruthless businessman," the lawman said. "He'll do anythin' he has to do to be successful."

"What does he own other than the saloon?"

"Nobody knows for sure," Haley said. "I'm sure he has people fronting for him. He could own half the town."

"And what about Letty Miller? Why did she want to be mayor?"

"She seems to be a woman who likes to be in charge," Haley said.

Clint had found that true of Letty, at least in bed.

"Seems to be?"

"At least, when it comes to this town," Haley said. "Even the council knuckles under to her when she wants something."

"Who else is in power in town?"

"Nobody, really," Haley said. "Oh, we've got some big ranchers out there, and some businessmen in town. We've got a cattlemen's club that doesn't allow women, except for Mayor Miller."

"I'll bet they love that."

"They wouldn't go against her by tryin' to keep her out," Haley said. "I think there's probably only one man in town who's not scared of her."

"And who's that?"

"Matt Fredericks," Haley said. "He's the editor of the newspaper, the Belle Fourche Gazette."

"I'd like to see some issues of that paper," Clint said. "It'd be very interesting."

"You can go to the Gazette office and talk to Fredericks," Haley said. "I'm sure he'd be willin' to show you some old copies."

"I think I'll do that," Clint said. "Do we have anything else to do?"

"Not today," Haley said. "Tomorrow morning we'll take a few men out for their shoot. Let's get together this evening for some final preparations. Meanwhile, you can do whatever you like."

"I think I'll finish this beer and then visit the newspaper office."

"Fine," Haley said. "I'll stay here and have another beer before I make some rounds."

Clint stood, said, "See you later," and left the saloon.

***

He found the newspaper office with no problem. He entered and, as with most newspaper offices, he found a man working on a printing press. When the man saw him, he turned, wiping his hands on a rag. He was short and squat, in his fifties, with steel grey hair.

"What can I do for you?"

"Are you Fredericks?"

"I am. And you?"

"Clint Adams."

The newspaper editor looked excited.

"The Gunsmith?"

"That's right."

"Hot damn!" Fredericks said. "I heard you in were in town. I was hopin' I'd get a chance to interview you."

"I'm afraid I'm not here for an interview, Mr. Fredericks," Clint said.

"Oh? Then what are you here for?"

"I wanted to get a look at some back editions of your paper."

"What for?"

"I'm curious to find out what some of the good and bad issues in your town are."

"I can tell you that," Fredericks said. "Right now, there are no good issues, and the worst is Mayor Miller."

Chapter Thirteen

"Can you explain that to me?" Clint asked.

"Sure," Fredericks said. "Come to my office. I could use a drink."

Clint followed the man down a long, narrow hallway to an office. There was barely room for a small wooden desk and chair. He sat in the chair, took a bottle of whiskey and two glasses out of a drawer.

"Drink?" he asked.

"Sure," Clint said, "a small one."

Fredericks poured the same amount into each glass and handed Clint one.

"So what do you need exactly, Mr. Adams?" he asked.

"The mayor," Clint reminded him.

"Oh, yeah," Fredericks said. "She's a hard bitch, pure and simple. She wanted the job of mayor, so she went out and got it."

"Wasn't she voted in?" Clint asked.

"It's easy to get votes when nobody's runnin' against you," the newspaperman said.

"And why didn't anybody run against her?"

"Because they were all scared of her."

"Why?"

"Because she's a scary bitch."

"That's the second time you called her a bitch," Clint said.

"Does that bother you?" Fredericks asked.

"Actually, yes, it does."

"Sorry," the man said, "I didn't know you were friends."

"We're not," Clint said. "I only met her when I first came to town."

"So why's it bother you?"

"I don't like hearing a woman being disrespected."

"Well," Fredericks said, "she doesn't exactly deserve respect."

"And why is that?"

Fredericks poured himself another drink. Clint hadn't touched his.

"She's kind of ruthless," he said. "Nobody wanted to take the chance they might beat her."

"From what I've heard," Clint said, "she pushed through this turkey shoot idea. That doesn't sound like the actions of a ruthless mayor."

"Nobody knows what she's really plannin'."

"You mean this shoot is going to lead to something else?"

"Could be," Fredericks said. "Why are you so interested in the whole thing?"

"She's asked me to run it."

"I thought the sheriff was supposed to run it," Fredericks said. "How's he feel about that?"

"We're running it together."

"Ah!" Fredericks said. "That's a surprise."

"Why?"

"Haley likes to work alone."

"This isn't work," Clint said. "It's a contest."

"Whatever you want to call it, Haley would usually like to do it alone. I suppose Mayor Miller convinced him to do this with you."

"She did."

"Then I don't suppose she'd object to me puttin' it in my paper."

"I wouldn't think so," Clint said, "since she expects my involvement to give the contest a higher profile."

"Good!" Fredericks finished his drink and returned the bottle to the drawer. "Then I have a new headline for tomorrow."

Clint was starting to realize he had made a mistake. If Fredericks plastered his name on a headline, it might attract some of the wrong people.

"You're thinking the wrong people might read of your involvement," Fredericks said, as if reading Clint's mind.

"That's true."

"You're not going to be here very long," the newspaperman went on. "It's only a two-day event. By the time somebody comes lookin' for you for the wrong reasons, you should be long gone."

"That's true enough."

Fredericks stood up.

"I better get my early edition started."

He walked Clint out to the front door.

"I'll be here until late," Fredericks said. "It'll take me a while to typeset this story. When I'm done, I usually end my day with a drink in the Deadwood. If I see you there, I'll buy you a drink."

"Suits me," Clint said. "You drink there because you know Kittredge?"

"I do know him," Fredericks said, "but I drink there because it's the best place in town."

"Then maybe I'll see you there."

Fredericks opened the door for him.

"By the way," Clint said, "you didn't tell me why you think the mayor is ruthless."

"I think you'll be findin' that out."

Clint went out the door.

"Oh, hey, you still want to look at those back issues?"

"I don't think so," Clint said. Like you said, I'm going to be finding out some things for myself."

Chapter Fourteen

Clint left the newspaper office, no wiser about Mayor Letty Miller. He was going to have to make up his mind about her, based on his own experiences. So far, his experiences had been very good. If all he was going to do was be with her, everything would be fine. But there were going to be plenty of other experiences to judge her on. It might yet prove to have been a mistake to stay in Belle Fourche. There was still a family named Sturdivant who lived about thirty miles north, who had invited him for Thanksgiving. He could still make it.

Clint went back to the South of Deadwood, which was in full swing. There was no room at the bar, and he didn't see any empty tables. He did, however, see Sheriff Haley sitting at one. He walked over to join the man.

"I thought you were making your rounds," Clint said.

"I did," Haley said. "And I'll make rounds again in a while. Meanwhile, I'll sit here. It's more comfortable than my office, don't you think?"

"I do," Clint said.

A saloon girl came over and Clint ordered two beers.

"Did you find out anything from Fredericks?" Haley asked.

"He seems to think Letty Miller is ruthless," Clint answered.

"Did he say why?"

"He seems to think I'll find out for myself."

"Hmm."

"Unless you want to tell me."

"I think everyone has their own ideas about that," the lawman said. "You will, too, eventually."

"So you're not going to tell me, either?"

"The woman is my boss," Haley said. "I'm not gonna be caught talkin' against her."

"Maybe," Clint said. "I should just ask her."

"Suit yourself."

The saloon girl came with the two fresh beers and set them down. They each picked theirs up and started to sip from them when Arthur Kittredge came over to the table.

"That's all, Millie," he told the saloon girl.

"You don't want a drink, boss?"

"No," he told her. "That's all."

"Yessir."

She turned and walked away, her heels clacking on the floor.

"I see you fellas got the schedule up for the turkey shoot contestants."

"Yes, we did," Clint said. "I didn't see your name on it."

"Oh, I won't be competing," Kittredge said. "I have my own plans for Thanksgiving."

"Good for you," Clint said. "Got a lady friend cooking for you?"

"Not a lady friend," Kittredge said. "Just a lady."

"Sounds perfect," Clint said.

"She can cook?"

Clint noticed that the sheriff was not eager to speak to Kittredge, who seemed to have the same sentiment.

"I wonder what the mayor had to offer the Gunsmith to get him to stay in town for the shoot?"

"She promised me a Thanksgiving dinner," Clint said. "That was a good enough incentive, since I was wondering what I was going to do for the holiday."

"Well," Kittredge said, "I hope it turns out to be worth your time."

As Kittredge walked away, Clint said to Haley, "You don't seem to like Mr. Kittredge."

"There's nothin' to like." He finished his beer and set the mug down. "It's gettin' late." He stood up. "I'll see you in the mornin'. We can meet at my office."

"I'll be there. Goodnight."

" 'night."

As Haley went out through the batwing doors, Clint waved at the saloon girl for another beer.

"Here you go, Mr. Adams," she said, setting it down.

"You know my name?"

"Everybody in town knows who you are," she said. "We're excited to have you here."

She was a pretty girl in her mid-twenties, with long, very dark hair.

"Your name is Millie, isn't it?"

"It is," she said, "most folks in town know me."

"How do you like working for Mr. Kittredge?"

"I don't," she said. "But the South of Deadwood pays more than any of the other places in town."

"Why don't you like him?" Clint asked. "Does he expect more of you?"

"Oh no, nothin' like that," she said. "He has his own women."

"Women?" Clint repeated. "Is he married?"

"No," she said, then leaned in and said, "but he likes other men's wives, and they like him."

"I see," Clint said. "And do the husbands know?"

"I don't think so," she said, then added, "if they did, I think one of them would kill him."

Someone across the room called to her and she said," 'scuse me."

He sipped his beer and watched her walk across the room.

Chapter Fifteen

Clint half expected Letty Miller to be in his room when he got there but found it very empty. He undressed, thinking about the turkey shoot the next day and wondered if he should just mount up in the morning and ride out? But he knew he wouldn't have been thinking that if Letty was in his bed. If it hadn't been for his desire for a good Thanksgiving dinner, he might not have stayed long enough for *that* to have happened.

He went to bed, committed to fulfilling his promise to officiate the shoot.

***

Clint woke early the next morning, had a quick breakfast in his hotel and went to the sheriff's office.

"You're five minutes late," Haley said, as he entered, "It's eight-oh-five."

"The contest starts at nine."

"Let's get our horses and ride out to the startin' point," Haley said.

They went to the livery together and saddled their animals. When they walked their horses out, Clint was surprised to find the lady mayor standing there. She was wearing riding clothes, but no hat.

"I wanted to wish you luck," she said.

"Why would *we* need luck?" Clint asked.

"I'm just hoping the event will go smoothly," she told him.

"It will," Sheriff Haley said, brusquely.

He rode off.

"The sheriff's a man of few words," Clint commented.

"He's not paid to talk," she said.

Clint touched the tip of his hat and rode after the lawman.

***

Clint caught up to the sheriff and, together, they rode to the designated starting point. There were already ten men there, several mounted, and others standing at their horse's head, holding the reins.

"Is everybody here?" Clint asked.

"The first shift, yes," Haley said.

They rode up to the crowd and dismounted. The mounted men did the same. All of them were holding rifles, except one man, who was holding a shotgun.

"Any turkey you shoot with that won't be worth eating," Clint pointed out.

"I'm not a very good shot," the older man said, "I thought I'd have a better chance of baggin' a turkey with this."

"Well," Clint said, "I doubt you'd have enough of a bird to put into a bag."

He left the man looking puzzled and went to stand next to the sheriff.

"We'll go out on foot. Make sure you leave space between each other. When you take a shot, you'll wait for me or Mr. Adams to check it. Is that understood?"

The ten men nodded.

"Then start your hunt!"

The men scattered, with none of them teaming up.

"Are we sure there are wild turkeys in this area?" Clint asked.

"Yes," Haley said. "They were seen hereabouts, recently. That's when the mayor came up with the idea of a shoot. Now we better move along, so we can observe."

They moved in the direction the men took, waiting for the sound of shots.

"What if they don't locate any birds?" Clint asked.

"Then the turkey shoot's a failure," the sheriff said, "and the mayor won't like that."

"Well, she'll still have the target shooting tomorrow," Clint offered.

"Yeah, but we need turkeys as prizes," Haley said. "Without them, we've got nothin'."

At that point they heard a volley of shots from somewhere off to the right. They went in that direction and found several men.

"I got one," a man said.

"No, I got it," another man said.

"Where?" Clint asked.

"Over there," one of the men pointed.

"Let's have a look," Haley said.

They went in the direction the man pointed and came across a large carcass. The men who had done the shooting came up behind them.

"So?" one man asked. "Did I get one?"

"No," another man said. "I got one."

"Seems you boys don't know the difference between a bird and a calf," Clint said, pointing.

The men looked down at the dead animal.

"I didn't shoot a calf," one man said.

"Neither did I," another man said.

"Well," Haley said, "one of you did. And you'll have to pay the owner."

"We better gather the men and warn them not to fire unless they're sure they're shooting a turkey," Clint suggested.

The sheriff sighed and said, "I didn't think we'd have to tell men that."

Chapter Sixteen

Clint and Sheriff Haley had to rule on several shootings during the course of the day and for different groups of men. Many of the shootings resulted in mangled birds, which would be used as prizes for the next day's target shooting. There were only three perfect neck shots which didn't do any damage to the body of the bird at all. Those men were able to take the bird home as their prize.

By the end of the day, the last of the shooters were coming in after having no luck.

"That's odd," Haley said.

"What is?" Clint asked.

"There's a man missing."

"Missing? Who?"

"His name's Sterling," Haley said. "You spoke to him early this mornin'."

"I did?"

Haley nodded.

"You criticized his choice of weapon. He was using a shotgun."

"Oh, an older man," Clint said.

"Older, and well known in town."

"How well known?"

"He was mayor for many years. When he stepped down, Mayor Miller took the job. Lately, though, he's been talkin' about runnin' for office again."

"Against the lady mayor?"

"Yep."

Clint looked at the sky.

"It's going to be dark soon. We should probably go out and see if we can find him."

"All the others have come in," Haley said. "We'll split up. You go that way, I'll go this way. If there's any trouble, fire two shots."

"Right."

The two men split up, covering most of the ground that had been used for the turkey hunt.

***

There was a knock on the back door of Arthur Kittredge's office. When he opened it, Kathleen Sterling slipped in.

"What are you doin' here?" he demanded, closing the door. "Someone could have seen you."

"You didn't mind last night," she said.

"That was my room, and it was late."

"Don't worry, no one saw me," she said, removing a scarf from her red hair.

"You're undeniable, Kathy," he told her. "Easy to see."

"I was careful," she said.

He went around behind his desk.

"Why are you here?"

"I think you know," she said, fiddling with the top button of her dress.

"Here? In my office? Where's your husband?"

"He's out hunting turkeys," she said and laughed. "He won't get one, not even with that shotgun he uses."

"What if he discovers you're not home when he gets there?" Kittredge asked.

"Arthur," she said, "you know he's not coming home."

"He's not supposed to come home from that hunt," Kittredge said. "That doesn't necessarily mean he won't."

"Don't worry, darling," she said. "Everything is arranged. It can't go wrong. Your Clint Adams will see to it."

At that moment the door to the saloon opened, and Millie, the saloon girl, walked in.

"Mr. Kittredge—" she started.

"Get out!" Kittredge yelled. "Next time knock!"

"Yessir."

She backed out.

"You think she heard anything?" Kathy asked.

"I don't think so. As for your husband coming home from the hunt, we'll find out soon enough. You better get along home."

She undid a second button.

"Are you sure?"

He came around from behind his desk, grabbed her by the shoulders, said, "Damn you!" and kissed her.

Chapter Seventeen

Clint found Walter Sterling. He came upon the man lying on his back in some bushes. His shotgun was lying nearby. Clint picked up the gun and checked it. It had not been fired. When he checked the body, he found that the man had been shot in the back, once.

Clint took out his revolver and fired it twice. He waited for the sheriff to appear.

"I found him like that," he said, pointing.

"Jesus," Haley said, looking down at the dead man. "Shot in the back. He never had a chance."

"From the looks of these tracks, it seems he was shot out in the open, and then dragged into these bushes."

"Who'd want to kill the old gent?" Haley wondered. He looked around. "Where's his shotgun?"

"It's over there," Clint said, pointing. "It hasn't been fired."

"Do you suppose he was shot by accident?"

"And then dragged out of sight to try and hide him?"

"The shooter could have panicked. After all, we had someone shoot a calf."

"No one could have mistaken this old man for a calf," Clint said.

"So you suppose it was deliberate, then."

"That's the way it looks to me."

"Well," Haley said, "we better get him back to town."

"Does he have a family?"

"A wife," Haley said. "She's much, much younger than he was."

"Is she going to be upset?"

"Probably not. Why don't you stay with the body? I'll be back with a wagon."

"That's fine."

"I won't be long."

When Haley left, Clint sat in the shadow of a nearby tree. He thought about who would have a motive for killing the old mayor. He didn't know many people in Belle Fourche, but he thought he might know someone with a motive. He hated to think it, but Letty Miller wouldn't want Walter Sterling to run against her in the next election. And he had already been told how ruthless she could be. But was she ruthless enough to have a man killed? That was a question he would have to ask when he got back to town. But of who?

That was another question.

***

He heard the sound of a wagon approaching and got to his feet. He saw Haley driving up with two other men.

"He's over there," Haley said. "Get him on the back of the buckboard."

"Yessir," one man said.

The two men lifted the dead man's body and laid it on the bed of the buckboard, then covered it with a blanket.

While Haley was gone Clint walked to where his Tobiano was and walked the horse back. Now he stood holding the horse's reigns as Sheriff Haley approached him.

"Did you spread the news in town?" Clint asked.

"I did."

"And?"

"And it's been suggested to me that you killed Sterling."

"Me? What reason would I have for killing a man I didn't even know?"

"For money. Why else would you be in Belle Fourche?" Haley asked.

"I don't sell my gun, Sheriff."

"For enough money, any man would sell his gun," Haley said.

"Not me."

"Then I'll need to take your gun until you can prove otherwise."

"Sheriff," Clint said, "I don't sell my gun, and I don't give it up."

"You're refusin' to give it to me?"

"I am," Clint said. "If you want it, you'll have to try to take it. And you'll need help."

The two men Haley brought with him were standing close by. When they heard these words, they shuffled their feet nervously.

"If you won't give up your gun, I'll ask you not to leave town until this matter is settled."

"And what does 'settled' mean?"

"Until we know who killed Mr. Sterling."

"And while I'm here, am I still officiating tomorrow's contest with you?"

"I suppose so," Haley said. "The mayor hasn't told me otherwise."

"Does she know about Sterling's death?"

"I don't think so," Haley said. I suppose I'll have to tell her later."

"I'll go with you, and we'll see if she wants to accuse me."

"Then we better get back."

It was getting dark when Clint mounted his horse and followed the buckboard back to town.

Chapter Eighteen

When they got to town, the two men stopped the buckboard in front of the undertakers. Clint and Haley rode to City Hall.

"Is she still going to be in her office?" Clint asked, as they dismounted.

"If she's not there we'll try her house. It's on the edge of town."

It turned out the building was locked, so they took their horses to the livery, and then Clint followed Haley to the mayor's house. It was a large, two-story wood-framed building standing off by itself.

When Haley knocked, Letty Miller answered.

"Well," she said, "if you're here for supper you're a little late. And besides, I only made enough for one."

"We're not here for supper, Miss Mayor," Haley said. "We have news of the shoot. Can we come in?"

"Of course." She stepped back to allow them to enter. "What is it? Didn't the shoot go well?"

Haley looked at Clint.

"There's no easy way to say this, Letty," Clint said. "A man was killed."

"Oh," she said. "By accident?"

"I don't think so," Clint said. "He was shot in the back, and the body was hidden."

"Who found it?"

"I did."

"How?"

"The sheriff said a man was missing. His name was Sterling. We went looking for him, and I found him."

"Vincent Sterling's dead?" she asked. "Shot in the back? Who would do that? Why?"

"That's for the sheriff to find out," Clint answered.

She looked at Haley.

"Who do you think did it, Sheriff?"

"I don't know."

"Well," she said, "like Clint says, you better find out."

"I will."

"Does Kathleen know?"

"Kathleen?" Clint asked.

"The young Mrs. Sterling," Letty told him.

"Not yet," Haley said. "Unless the word's gotten around."

"Well, you have to go and tell her."

"I will."

"Then go! Now!"

After Haley went out the door, Letty looked at Clint and said, "You look like you could use a drink."

"I could, thanks."

She poured two glasses of whiskey and handed him one.

"What's goin' on between you and the sheriff?" she asked.

"He tried to take my gun."

"He did? I didn't think he had it in him."

"Well," Clint said, "he asked me for it, and I said he'd have to take it."

"I see," she said. "Why'd he want it?"

"He said he thought maybe I killed Sterling."

"Why would you do that?"

"According to him, for money."

"And who would hire you to kill that old man?"

"I don't know," Clint said, "but somebody suggested it to Haley."

"You didn't do it, did you, Clint?"

"No," he said, "my gun's not for sale."

"Then you've got nothin' to worry about," she said. "Haley is no detective."

"Then who's going to find out who killed him?"

"Maybe you could."

"I'm no detective, either," Clint said. "I agreed to stay in town for the turkey shoot, and then I'm on my way."

"Do you think that'll be all right with the sheriff?" she asked.

"I don't know," Clint said. "He'd have to get up the nerve to try and stop me. Or enough men."

She laughed.

"I think that's somethin' I'd like to see."

"Well, I wouldn't." He put the empty glass down. "Thanks for the drink."

"Aren't you stayin'?" she asked.

"I've been out there all day," he said. "I need a meal and some rest, and I've got an early day tomorrow."

"You're still going to do the turkey shoot?"

"I said I would," he replied, "and I keep my word."

"And the sheriff knows you'll be there?"

"He knows."

"Well, I hope he doesn't get his nerve up tomorrow and ruin the contest."

She walked him to the door.

"If you want to come back later tonight," she said, "come ahead. You might be safer here than in your hotel room."

"I'll keep that in mind."

He left and she closed the door behind him. When she returned to the living room, Arthur Kittredge was coming down the stairs.

"I told you Haley wouldn't have the gumption to arrest Adams."

"We still have time," she said. "Meanwhile, you better get out of here in case Adams comes back."

"I'll go," Kittredge said, "but he won't be back. I don't think you have as tight a grip on him as you think."

She laughed and said, "We'll see."

Chapter Nineteen

After a steak at the café, Clint went to the South of Deadwood Saloon. The inside was bright, alive and warm. He unbuttoned his jacket and went to the crowded bar.

"Beer," he told the bartender.

"Here, or a table?"

Clint looked around the crowded interior.

"Is there one available?"

"Millie will find you one," he said, waving.

The pretty saloon girl hurried over.

"You're back!"

"He needs a table," the bartender said.

"This way," she said, grabbing Clint's left arm. He snatched his beer from the bar as she tugged him away.

She pulled him through the crowd until they reached an empty table.

"This is for you," she said.

"You knew I was coming back?"

She smiled and said, "I had a feeling."

He sat.

"Why was this table empty?"

"That's easy," she said. "It's the boss's private table."

"Is he going to like me sitting here?"

"You can ask 'im when he comes out," she said. "My money's on you, Mr. Adams."

"Just call me Clint, Millie."

"Let me know if you want another one, Clint," she said, and hurried away.

There were two other girls working the floor, but they stayed away from Clint. He wondered if Millie had warned them off.

Millie brought Clint a second beer, and before he finished it, Arthur Kittredge came out of his office. He saw Clint sitting at his table and walked over.

"I hope you don't mind," Clint said. "It was the only one available. If you want me to move—"

"No, that's fine," Kittredge said. "You mind if I join you?"

"It's your table."

Kittredge sat and waved at Millie to come over.

"Bring me a beer and Mr. Adams a fresh one."

"Yes, sir."

When she returned with them and set them down Kittredge asked her, "Did you decide to seat Mr. Adams at my table?"

"Yessir," she said, standing primly—waiting to be scolded.

"Good girl," he said. "That's all"

She walked away, slowly this time.

"How did the shoot go today?" he asked.

"You haven't heard?"

"Heard what?"

"A man was killed," Clint said. "His name was Sterling."

"Walter Sterling's dead?" Kittredge asked. "How did it happen?"

"He was shot in the back."

"By accident?"

"It doesn't seem so," Clint said. "After he was shot, his body was dragged into some brush."

"My God," Kittredge said. "Who'd do such a thing?"

"I don't know," Clint said. "I don't know enough people in town to guess. The sheriff seemed to think I might've been hired to do it."

"And you weren't?"

"I don't hire my gun out," Clint told him. "And if I did, I'd never backshoot a man."

"Not for any amount of money?"

"Exactly."

"Everybody is supposed to have a price."

"I don't," Clint said. "Not for murder."

"So what are you going to do?"

"What the mayor asked me to do," Clint replied. "I'll officiate the rest of this contest."

"With the sheriff?"

"Yes."

"Even though he suspects you?"

"I don't know that he really does," Clint said. "It was just an idea."

"He won't go up against you anyway," Kittredge said. "Not without help."

"Let me ask you something," Clint said.

"Go ahead."

"I've been told Sterling was once mayor and might have had his eye on the job again."

"Some people think—or thought that."

"And how did Mayor Miller feel about that?"

"She wasn't afraid of him," Kittredge said. "If you're suggesting she had him killed—"

"I'm just asking questions," Clint said, cutting him off. "Let me ask you another one."

"Go on."

"Who do *you* think killed him? Or had him killed? You know the people of this town."

"I might make a few guesses," Kittredge said, "but I'd have to think about it first." He finished his beer and stood up. "Use the table as long as you like. Goodnight."

"Goodnight."

Instead of going back to his office, Kittredge went to the stairs and went up. Clint assumed he lived on the second floor.

When Kittredge was gone Millie hurried over.

"We have to talk," she said.

"Then sit."

"No, not here," she said, hurriedly. "I'll come to your hotel later."

Before Clint could say anything else, she hurried away.

Chapter Twenty

Clint finished his beer and went to his hotel to wait for Millie. He pulled off his boots, hung his gunbelt on the bedpost, and sat in the single armchair in the room. When the knock came on the door a couple of hours later, he had been drifting off. He grabbed his gun from his holster and went to the door.

"Let me in, quickly," Millie hissed. He backed up, allowed her to enter, and closed the door.

"What's this all about?" he asked her.

She was still wearing the dress she wore in the saloon. The wrap she had over her bare shoulders had done little to protect her against the cold. Her pale skin was dappled with goose bumps.

"Here," he said, pulling the blanket from the bed and wrapping it around her.

"Thank you."

"Sit in this chair," he said. "I've been in it for hours and it's warm."

She lowered herself into the chair and said, "You're right. You have a warm body."

Clint sat on the end of the bed.

"What's this about, Millie?" he asked. "Why did we have to talk here?"

"I don't want anyone to see us together outside the saloon," she said.

"Why?"

"I could get into trouble for talking to you."

"With who?"

"Mr. Kittredge."

"So you want to talk to me about him?"

"I want to warn you about him," Millie said. "He's planning something, and it has to do with you."

"How do you know that?"

"I went into his office when he was talking to someone about you. He stopped talking and yelled at me to get out. But I heard your name."

"When was this?"

"Yesterday."

"And who was he talking to?"

"A woman," she said. "Kathleen Sterling."

"Sterling?"

"Yes," she said, "the old mayor's young wife."

"What exactly did you hear?"

"Just your name."

"From him?"

Millie shook her head, "Her," she said. "He threw me out so fast I knew something must be wrong."

"Well," Clint said, "thanks, Millie. I'll keep that in mind."

She wrapped herself more tightly in the blanket, her hands moving beneath it.

"Is there anything else?"

"I'm still very cold, and since you have such a warm body, I was hoping you could help me."

She stood up and something dropped to the floor. He looked down and saw that it was her dress. Now he knew what her hands had been doing beneath the blanket.

"Millie—"

"You're not going to let me be cold," she asked, shrugging off the blanket, "are you?"

She was completely naked, a lovely young woman with slim hips, tea-cup sized breasts, tipped with coral-colored nipples. As powerful looking as Letty Miller was naked, Millie looked soft and supple. Luckily, Clint appreciated women of all sizes and shapes.

"It wouldn't be polite," Millie added.

"No," he said, "I suppose it wouldn't be."

"And I'd especially feel the warmth of your body if you were naked."

"Of course," he said. "Where are my manners?"

He began to undress . . .

***

Letty Miller was disappointed when Clint didn't re-appear at her door after several hours. Her decision to use him during the turkey shoot had nothing to do with her plans to take him to her bed again, more than once, before discarding him.

Apparently, he had found something else he would rather do tonight than come back to her. And since she had already sent Art Kittredge home, she was destined to spend the night alone. That didn't make her happy at all.

***

When Clint was naked, he took Millie's naked form into his arms and held her close. Her hard nipples scraped his skin pleasantly.

"Ah yes," she moaned, pressing her lips to his chest, "so warm, just as I knew you would be."

Chapter Twenty-One

Clint lifted Millie, surprised at how light she was, and carried her to the bed. She kissed and nibbled at his neck, and when he set her down on the sheets, she stretched out and smiled.

He slipped into bed with her, gathered her up into his arms again, and kissed her. Her mouth opened beneath his, anxiously. He slid one hand down her body until his hand was between her thighs, where he found her already wet. He leaned over to take her nipples in his mouth, while inserting his middle finger into her. She gasped, grabbed for his head and closed her thighs around his hand.

"Ooh God . . ." she groaned.

He continued to kiss his way down her body until he could replace his hand with his mouth and tongue. He worked on her until she was gushing, soaking the sheets beneath them, and then removed his mouth, mounted her and drove his penis deep inside her steamy hot depths . . .

***

"Omigod!" she gasped, moments after he rolled off of her.

"Are you warm, enough now?" he asked.

"Hot," she said, "I'm very hot, thank you."

"I guess I can't send you out into the cold night," he commented.

"Oh," she said, sitting up quickly, "I can't stay!"

"Why not?"

"I have a room over the saloon. They'll be wondering where I am." She quickly got off the bed and grabbed her dress and wrap from the floor.

"But it's cold out," he reminded her.

"I was lying," she said, "I was never cold. I'm used to this weather." Pulling on her dress she added, "I'll be fine." She covered her shoulders with her wrap, then turned to look at him. "But if you're in town tomorrow night, I'd like to sneak over here again."

"Be my guest," he said. "I'll probably be here at least one more night."

"Will you watch out for Mr. Kittredge?"

"Oh," he said, "I'll definitely have my eye on Kittredge. I'm also going to see the widow Sterling."

"You'll definitely have to watch out for her, then," Millie said. "She's bound to try to get you into her bed."

"I'll be careful."

"I hope so," Millie said. "Will I see you at the saloon tomorrow?"

"I'm sure you will."

"Goodnight, then." She opened the door, then turned to look at him. "It was wonderful!"

And she was gone . . .

***

Clint woke the next morning, laid there for a moment with his hands behind his head, still naked. He replayed the activities of the night before, and realized he wished Millie had stayed the night. But he wouldn't have wanted to get her in trouble.

He got out of bed, washed up, and then dressed. He strapped on his gun, and then slipped into his fur-lined jacket. Unlike Millie, he wasn't used to this South Dakota weather.

He left the hotel and returned to the café he had eaten in before and had a good, hot breakfast plate of bacon-and-eggs-and spuds. He got to the starting point of the day's target shoot in plenty of time.

"I wasn't sure you'd show up," Sheriff Haley said.

"I said I would," he replied. "I wasn't sure you'd go ahead with this part, given what happened yesterday."

"Sterling may be dead," Haley said, "but these folks still want their turkey."

"How did the widow take the news?"

"She said 'Oh dear,' but didn't shed a single tear," Haley said.

"I'm going to stop in and see her when we're finished here."

"That's up to you," Haley said. "We better get this thing going."

The contest was being held in an empty lot in the center of town. Targets had been set up at one end.

"Why's this area right here in the middle of town?" Clint asked.

"It was a saloon, but it burned down."

"It's a prime location," Clint said. "Why did nobody rebuild?"

"The owner was inside when it burned," Haley said. "Ownership of the property is up in the air."

"Well, somebody gave their permission to use it," Clint observed.

"That would be the mayor," Sheriff Haley said. "Her word is law."

Chapter Twenty-Two

The targets were bullseyes drawn on flat boards nailed to wooden posts. Before the contest even started, Clint was hearing men complaining that the targets were too far away.

"Nobody could hit a bullseye from here," one man complained.

"Oh, Jesus," Haley said.

Clint stepped forward.

"Anybody who doesn't want to shoot can leave now," he called out.

Another man turned toward him and complained, "A shot from this distance can't be done."

There were five bullseye targets. Clint drew his gun and fired five times. Each bullet went right in the center. One of the men ran to the targets and inspected each one.

"Dead center, every one!" he shouted.

"And that was with a pistol," Clint said, reloading. "All of you will be shooting with rifles." He holstered his gun. "Any more complaints?"

There was some grumbling, but no complaints.

"Sheriff," Clint said, "over to you."

Clint stepped back and allowed the sheriff to take charge. They had several rather mangled turkeys left from the day before, which would be given out as prizes. It was assumed that there were women in town who could clear the bird carcasses of lead and cook them into decent Thanksgiving meals. And they wouldn't have had to spend a penny on them.

Clint watched the shooting for a while, and it seemed the disgruntled men had a point. No one was able to hit a target from that distance.

Once again Clint stepped forward and spoke, this time to the sheriff.

"Haley," he said, "I suggest you move these men closer, or we may never finish here."

"You have a point."

The sheriff announced that each man should take ten steps forward and shoot again. They did. There were still no bullseyes, but a couple of men did actually hit the target.

One-by-one the men began to be eliminated. It finally came down to five.

"How many turkeys do we have as prizes?" Clint asked Sheriff Haley.

"Three," the lawman said. "There was nothing left of the others."

"Right. Do you mind?"

"Be my guest," Haley said, and stepped back.

"All right," Clint announced, "no more bullseye. The three closest shots will win the turkeys."

"That's not fair," one man said.

"It's getting late," Clint said. "Do you want to shoot in the dark?"

None of the five men wanted that. Two of them were town businessmen in their fifties, two were ranch hands in their thirties, and the fifth was a young, newly married man in his twenties who desperately wanted to give his young bride a turkey for Thanksgiving. Clint learned all this from the sheriff before letting the five men shoot.

"One at a time," he told them. "You'll shoot at the same target. The three closest to the bullseye will win the turkeys."

"This is silly," one of the businessmen said, sourly.

"Make your point by coming closest," Clint told him.

Clint could see how nervous the young man was, so he was going to allow him to shoot last.

"You first," he told the sour man.

The man took a step forward, raised his rifle, sighted, and fired. One of the men Haley had used to bring Sterling's body back to town was standing near the targets. He was acting as spotter. He went to the target, then waved.

"What's that mean?" the sour man asked. "Was I close?"

"You'll find out after you've all shot," Clint said to him. He pointed to the other businessman. "You next."

The man stepped forward, sighted and fired. The spotter waved.

Clint had the two ranch hands go next, and then he pointed to the young husband.

"Now you."

Nervously, the young man took a step, raised his rifle, and Clint could see his hand shaking.

"Wait!"

The young man lowered his rifle.

Clint moved closer to him, so only he could hear what Clint had to say.

"Hey!" the sour man yelled to Haley. "He can't help him!"

"He's just tryin' to keep the boy from shootin' himself in the foot, Mr. Yates. Now step back."

Grumbling, the man did so.

Clint patted the young man on the back and then moved away.

"Now take your shot," he said.

The young man raised his rifle, sighted and fired. The spotter waved.

Clint walked to the target and the spotter pointed five times. Clint walked back to the five men.

"You," he said, pointing to one of the ranch hands, "you," pointing to the other, "and you," pointing to the young man. "You three have won your turkey." He looked at the two businessmen. "Sorry, gents."

"Hey," the sour man snapped, "I want to see those targets."

"Sorry," Clint said, "they've already been taken down."

"This isn't right," the man complained to the sheriff.

"You two can afford to buy a turkey," Clint said. "The contest is over." He looked at the three winners. "You can pick your turkeys up at the café."

The two ranch hands were very satisfied.

The young man came over to Clint and said, "Thanks a lot, Mr. Adams."

"You're welcome."

The young man hurried after the ranch hands, and the three men went to collect their prizes. The two businessmen slunk away unhappily.

Haley turned to Clint and asked, "What did you say to that young fella? His hands weren't shakin' at all when he took his last shot."

Clint smiled.

"I told him to relax and take his shot," Clint said. "I assured him that, even if he missed the target completely, I was awarding him a turkey."

Haley raised his eyebrows.

"You cheated Mr. Yates and Howard?"

"I did, indeed," Clint said. "Like I told them, they could afford to buy a turkey. Those other three couldn't."

"So who actually won?"

Clint smiled and said, "I'll never tell."

Chapter Twenty-Three

It was getting dark as Clint and Haley walked back toward the sheriff's office.

"What's next for you?" the sheriff asked.

"I assume you still don't want me to leave town?" Clint asked.

"That's right."

"Then I'm going to have a meal," Clint said, "and visit Mrs. Sterling."

"What're you gonna say to her?" Haley asked.

"I don't know," Clint said. "I suppose I want to see how bereft she is about her husband's death."

"Nobody in town knows why she bothered to marry him," Haley said, as they reached his office, "but she sure as hell didn't love him."

"Do they know at the café to give our three winners their turkeys?"

"They know."

"I'll go there for my meal anyway."

"There are better places to eat," Haley said.

"I know, the mayor took me to one," Clint said. "But I like that café."

"Then I'll see you tomorrow," Haley said.

"Tomorrow's Thanksgiving," Clint reminded him.

"I don't have any family," Haley said. "I'll be here."

"Well, the mayor promised me a turkey dinner," Clint said, "but I'm not counting on it. See you tomorrow, Sheriff."

Haley went into his office, and Clint walked to the café.

***

By the time Clint got to the café, the three men had picked up their birds. He sat at the same table as his previous visits and ordered a steak.

It was after suppertime, and many of the tables were empty. There were only men who stayed late at work who were having a late meal.

"Your three winners came in for their bird," the waiter said to Clint.

"Good."

"That young feller was real excited about bringin' his wife a turkey for Thanksgiving."

"What are you going to be doing for Thanksgiving?" Clint asked.

"We'll be open most of the day. After closing, the cook and me will go home to our wives and our Thanksgiving dinners."

"Sounds good."

"Not so good," the man said. "You ain't never had my wife's cookin'. That bird's gonna be dry as the desert."

The waiter went back to the kitchen, shaking his head.

Clint finished his meal, paid his bill, then left to go to the widow Sterling's house, except he realized he didn't know where she lived.

He wondered if the sheriff would still be in his office? He would certainly know where she lived. He walked over there, found the office locked and dark. He decided to go to the South of Deadwood Saloon and see if Millie knew where the widow lived.

***

At that moment, Millie was in Art Kittredge's office. She was on her knees in front of her boss, who had a tight, painful hold on her wrist.

"P-please, Mr. Kittredge," she said, "you're hurting me."

"I mean to, Millie," he said. "All you have to do to get me to stop is tell me why you went to Clint Adams hotel last night."

Millie didn't want to answer her boss' question but thought the best course of action might be to tell him the truth.

"H-he's the Gunsmith," she said. "I-I went there t-to sleep with him."

"That's all?"

"He has a r-reputation," she said. "I-I wanted t-to see if it was true."

"And was it?"

"Y-yes, sir," she said. "It was."

He released her wrist and she slumped to the floor, holding it.

"Go back to work!" he snapped.

"Y-yessir."

She got herself up off the floor and went out the door to the saloon.

Chapter Twenty-Four

Clint entered the saloon and went straight to the bar. Crowded, as usual, a few men recognized him and made room.

"Beer," he told the bartender.

"A table?" the man asked, as he set the beer down.

"Not tonight," Clint said. "Is Millie around?"

"In with the boss."

They both looked at the door to Kittredge's office, and at that moment it opened and Millie came stumbling out cradling an arm. Clint rushed over to her.

"Are you all right?" he asked.

"I'm fine," she said. "It'll take more than bending my wrist—"

"I'll show Kittredge how to bend a wrist—" Clint started, but she stopped him by putting her hand against this chest. "Not now. Let's sit."

She guided him to a table that wasn't Kittredge's, and the bartender brought his beer over as they sat.

"What did he want from you?" Clint asked.

"He knew I was in your hotel last night," she said. "He wanted to know why."

"And what did you tell him?"

"The truth," she said. "That I went to your room to sleep with you."

"And how did he take that?"

"It didn't bother him," she said. "See, I'm not married, and he likes other men's wives."

"Like Mrs. Sterling?"

"Yes," she said, "Kathleen Sterling was one of his favorites."

"Was?"

"Well, yes," she said. "After all, her husband's dead, so she's not married anymore."

"That reminds me why I came here," Clint said. "I don't know where the widow lives."

"Go out the door, turn right and walk six streets. The Sterling house is bigger than Mayor Millers."

"Is it, now?"

"Yes, and the mayor wants it. I'm sure people have told you she gets what she wants."

"Oh, yes."

"Are you going to see Kathleen Sterling tonight?"

"That was my plan. Will you be all right?"

"I'll be fine," she said, "and if you want me to, I'll come to you tonight."

"That suits me." He stood up, and she followed.

"I have to get back to work," she said. "And remember, be careful of that Sterling woman."

"I'll be very careful," he said, and left the saloon.

***

He found the Sterling house and saw what Millie had said was true. It was much larger than the mayor's and Clint could see why a woman like Letty Miller would want such a house. But would she have the old mayor killed to get it?

That was something he would have to talk to Letty about, but right now he was going to talk to Kathleen Sterling.

The house stood off by itself, with no neighbors close enough to hear even a scream. He went up the walk to the front door and knocked. The door was opened by an impossibly beautiful woman in her twenties, with golden blonde hair. She was wearing a black dress, which he assumed was because she was in mourning.

"Yes?" she asked. "What do you want?"

"I want to talk to you if you're Mrs. Sterling."

"I'm Kathleen Sterling," she said. "Who are you?"

"My name's Clint Adams. I'm the one who found your husband's body."

"Oh!" Her curious blue eyes suddenly became very wide and innocent. He was sure she had used that look on many men.

"Won't you come in?" she asked, backing up.

"Thank you."

She closed the door behind him and said, "Come this way."

She led him to a plushy furnished sitting room with a large window that looked out on the front yard.

"Can I offer you a drink?" she asked. "Whiskey? Or coffee?"

"Coffee, if it's no bother."

"It's no bother," she said, "We—I—have a cook. I'll be right back. Make yourself comfortable.

She left him alone, and he looked around at the expensive furnishings. It seemed as if the old politician was not averse to lining his own pockets. And now the young widow was well off, if not rich.

She returned to the room, empty-handed.

"The cook is bringing the coffee," she said. "Please, sit."

She sat on the plush sofa, and he chose the matching armchair.

"I'm very grateful to you, Mr. Adams, for finding my husband's body and bringing him home."

"It seemed the least I could do."

"Well," she said, "I think the least you could do is find out who killed him."

He was about to reply when a heavyset woman in her fifties entered the room carrying a tray.

Chapter Twenty-Five

Clint accepted a cup of coffee from the woman's tray, and then she withdrew.

"Mrs. Sterling," he said to the young widow, "I'm afraid it's the sheriff's job to find out who killed your husband."

"That man is useless," she said. "But it doesn't matter. I know who killed Walter."

"Oh? And who's that?"

"Our lady mayor," she said. "She didn't want him running against her. She knew he'd beat her. And, oh yeah, she wants this house."

"I'm sure your husband must've left you this house, and all his property."

"She'll try to buy it from me," Kathleen Sterling said.

"Do you want to sell it?" Clint asked.

"I don't know," the woman said. "I guess that will depend on her offer. Or my mood when she makes it." She leaned forward and picked up a cup from the tray the cook had left on the coffee table. "But tell me, Mr. Adams, why did you come here?"

"I felt I should come and pay my respects," he said. "I'm sorry it's taken me this long."

"I'm sure you've been very busy," Kathy Sterling said. "And you must have plans for Thanksgiving, tomorrow."

"Not really," he said. "I stayed in town to officiate the turkey shoot with the sheriff. The mayor promised me a Thanksgiving dinner, but from what people have been telling me, I'm not sure I can trust her to keep her promise."

"Well, we had plans for cook to make a special dinner tomorrow," Kathleen said. "I'm sure my husband would want us to go forward with it, so you'd be welcome to come here and eat. Our cook is very good."

"Doesn't she have her own family?"

"My husband was her only family," Kathleen said. "She's lived in with him for over twenty years. When I moved in, we asked her to stay."

"Will she stay now that your husband is dead?" Clint asked.

"I don't know," she said. "I suppose that's a discussion we'll have to have."

"Will there be a funeral?"

"My husband has already been buried," she said. "He always told me if something happened, don't waste time."

"I see. And what about Mr. Kittredge, over at the South of Deadwood Saloon?"

"What about him?"

"I heard you and he were friends."

"Really?" she asked. "Who could have told you that?"

"It's just something I heard."

"Well, you heard wrong," she said. "My husband knew Mr. Kittredge, of course, but I barely know him."

He sipped his coffee and put the cup down.

"Can I ask you something, Mrs. Sterling?"

"You can if you'll call me Kathy."

"Kathy," he said, "how did you come to be married to a man so much older than you?"

She smiled and said, "He asked me, and I figured, why not? I didn't have any better offers."

"I guess that makes as much sense as anything," Clint said. "Is there anything else I can do for you, Kathy?"

She looked him up and down and the innocent eyes became something else entirely.

"Mr. Adams," she said, "I'll give that some thought and let you know."

She walked him to the front door.

"Don't forget," she told him, "you have an open invitation for Thanksgiving."

"I'll keep it in mind," he said. "Goodnight."

"Goodnight, Mr. Adams."

"Clint."

"Goodnight, Clint."

He left and she closed the door behind him and breathed a sigh of relief.

The cook, Bertha, came in to pick up the cups and the tray.

"I invited Mr. Adams to Thanksgiving dinner tomorrow, Bertha," Kathleen said. "He's a stranger in town and has nowhere else to go."

"I am cookin' because we have so much food," Bertha told her. "He found the Mister, so he is welcome."

"Bertha," Kathy said, "I always wanted to ask you, why did you call my husband 'the Mister?'" You were with him for so many years."

"I worked for him," she said. "I always thought I must treat him with respect."

"Come on, Bertha," Kathy said. "Did you love him?"

Bertha curled her lip and said, "You are disgusting."

Kathy laughed.

"After Thanksgiving dinner, I will be leaving. I won't cook for you anymore."

"And going where?" Kathy asked.

"I don't rightly know," Bertha said, "Just away from you."

She walked toward the kitchen.

"That's just fine with me," Kathy called after her. "I don't need you, anymore!"

Chapter Twenty-Six

Clint returned to his hotel room, kicked off his boots, removed his gunbelt, and gave his position some thought.

Kathleen Sterling hadn't given any indication that she was a grieving widow. He had no way of knowing what her next move would be. And, of course, he had to wonder if it was she who had her husband killed. According to Millie, Kathy Sterling knew Arthur Kittredge, while she claimed to not know him at all.

Clint realized he had fulfilled his promise to Letty Miller about officiating her turkey shoot. He would be well within his rights to ride out of town on Thanksgiving Day and head for dinner with the Sturdivant family. If there was one thing keeping him from doing that, it was the fact that Sterling had been shot in the back.

Ever since his friend Wild Bill Hickok had been shot in the back in nearby Deadwood, he had hated back-shooters. He did not feel he could ride off and allow someone to get away with shooting Walter Sterling in the back. Also, the fact that Deadwood was so close to Belle Fourche simply intensified the feeling.

So he was committed to staying in town until he found the culprit and made him—or her—pay.

If a woman was behind Sterling's murder, it had to be either the wife, or the mayor. It seemed clear neither woman had any love for the man.

Then there was Arthur Kittredge, who seemed to have a penchant for other men's wives, including Kathleen Sterling. Did he want her badly enough to have her husband killed? Or was she just one of many such conquests? Of course, there was also the fact that Kathleen was now a rich widow. Maybe that put her at the top of Kittredge's list.

Clint knew of only one person in town who might be able to supply him with information he needed. The sheriff was out. It seemed to Clint that the lawman was under the lady mayor's thumb. Also, he didn't seem to have the gumption that was needed for murder. That left only Millie to give Clint some help. He simply didn't know anyone else in town who might talk to him. He had only had dealings with a waiter and a bartender, and he didn't think either of them would be willing to help. Of course, all he needed was some gossip, and who would have more of that than a bartender or waiter?

But for the time being—and since she had promised to come to his room tonight—Millie seemed the most likely source.

He settled back on the bed to wait for Millie to arrive. As it got later and later, it seemed clear she wasn't coming, so he set aside the Mark Twain he was reading and went to sleep.

***

When he entered the café the next morning, there seemed a lot of conversation going on between tables. He was lucky to grab what he now thought of as his regular table, since the place was fairly crowded.

When the waiter came over, he asked, "What's all the buzzing about?"

"One of the saloon girls from the Deadwood got killed last night."

Clint felt a cold rock form in the pit of his stomach.

"Which one?" he asked.

"A nice girl, name of Millie."

Now the coldness spread to his whole body.

"How was she killed?"

"Somebody strangled her and left her in an alley."

"Where?"

"Somewhere between here and the saloon."

She was on her way to meet with him. He stood up.

"Not eatin'?" the waiter asked.

"I've lost my appetite," Clint said, and rushed out.

***

When Clint burst into the sheriff's office. Sheriff Haley looked up in surprise.

"What the—" he started, but Clint cut him off.

"Do you have any idea who killed Millie?" he demanded.

"Oh, you heard," Haley said. "No, I don't. She was found this morning in an alley—"

"What about Kittredge?" Clint demanded.

"Why would Kittredge kill a girl who worked for him?" the lawman asked.

"She walked in on him when he was talking to Kathleen Sterling," Clint said. "She heard them saying my name."

"Why would that mean he had anything to do with killing her?"

"I think they were planning her husband's murder."

"And why mention you?"

"I think they wanted to frame me for it."

"That's a stretch, ain't it?"

"Didn't you accuse me of doing it?"

Haley looked uncomfortable.

"I just said that was a possibility," he said. "After all, you have a reputation—"

"Not as a hired killer," Clint said, cutting him off.

"That's true, but a fast man with a gun."

"Not a backshooter. Who told you to accuse me? Was it Kittredge? Or the mayor?"

"Why would the mayor do that?"

"I think she saw me as a means to an end," Clint said, although he was still not sure he believed it himself. "Get rid of the old mayor and blame it on me."

If you believe that of her, you'll have to take it up with her."

"Right now, I'm more concerned with Millie's murder."

"Her killer could've been a cowboy whose advances she resisted," Haley said.

"I doubt that," Clint said. "It'd be too much of a coincidence."

"So you suspect Kittredge?"

"Yes."

"Then take that up with him," Haley said. "I have to have more of an open mind about it."

"Do you suspect it's connected to Sterling's death?" Clint asked.

"No," Haley said, "I don't see that."

"Then you're either a fool," Clint said, "or you're involved."

"I think you better leave, Mr. Adams," Haley said. "I have work to do."

"If I find out you were involved in either murder," Clint said, "I'll be back."

"You're not leaving town?"

"Not until I find out who killed Sterling and Millie."

He turned and stormed out.

Chapter Twenty-Seven

Clint decided to confront those he felt might be responsible for Millie's, or Sterling's, death. He wanted them to know he wasn't going anywhere until he found out who did it.

When he got to the South of Deadwood, the front door was locked. He pounded his fist until the bartender opened the door.

"We're not open," the man said.

"I want to see Kittredge," Clint said.

"About what?"

"Millie."

The bartender's face fell.

"That poor girl."

"Are you going to let me in?"

"Why do you wanna see the boss?"

"To ask him if he killed Millie."

The bartender looked surprised.

"Why would you ask him that?"

"Because I want an answer. Now, let me in. Don't make me force my way."

The bartender said, "Come ahead," and stood aside.

"Where is he? His office?"

"Yeah," the bartender said, closing and locking the door.

Clint walked across the empty saloon floor and stormed into Kittredge's office without bothering to knock.

Kittredge looked up from his desk in surprise.

"What the—"

"If you had anything to do with Millie's death, I'll make you pay, Kittredge!"

"What the hell are you talking about?" Kittredge countered. "Why would I kill a girl who works for me."

"You tell me."

Kittredge stood and said, "I wouldn't. Why would I?"

"She was afraid of you."

"I was her boss. She's supposed to be afraid of me."

"She was afraid you were planning to do something to me," Clint said. "She wanted to warn me but didn't want you to know. I guess you did."

"You're crazy!" Kittredge said.

"She walked in on you and the Sterling woman talking about me."

"I don't know what she thought she heard—"

"Look, Kittredge, I'm just here to warn you," Clint said, cutting him off. "If I find out I'm right about you, I'm coming for you."

Clint didn't wait for a response. He turned and stormed out.

The bartender was waiting for him at the door. He unlocked it and opened it.

"Mr. Adams, do you really think Mr. Kittredge had somethin' to do with Millie's death?"

"I'm having a hard time coming up with somebody else," Clint said. "The sheriff seems to think it was an unhappy cowboy she turned away."

"Millie never got anybody that mad," the bartender said. "I doubt that was it."

"What do you think about your boss?" Clint asked.

"He's a hard man," the bartender said. "But I don't know that he's a killer."

Time for some gossip, Clint thought.

"What do you think of Kittredge and the mayor? What's their relationship?"

"I ain't never even seen them together," the barman said. "But Mr. Kittredge favors married women, and the mayor ain't married."

"So you've seen him with Mrs. Sterling.?"

"Oh, yeah," the man said. "Him and that young wife—definitely."

"How do you feel about Kittredge killing Sterling?"

"I don't see it," the man said. "Not over his wife, an-yway."

"What other reason?"

"They didn't see eye-to-eye, and Sterling was talkin' about runnin' for mayor again. Mr. Kittredge wouldn't have liked it."

"Would he kill him to keep him out of office?"

The man gave that some thought and then said, "I don't see that, either."

"What about the lady mayor?"

"Now that woman," the bartender said, "would do anythin' to get what she wanted."

"Okay," Clint said, "thanks."

He went out and the bartender closed the door behind him.

Chapter Twenty-Eight

The next person to confront was the mayor. He headed for City Hall, figuring at this time of day she would be in her office.

As he burst into her office, she sat back in her chair behind her desk, and smiled at him.

"You didn't come back last night," she said. "I waited a long time before going to bed. If you want to make up for it now, you'll have to lock the door."

"Did you hear about the saloon girl who was found dead this morning?" he asked.

"Yes, I did," she said. "Terrible thing. I told the sheriff to clear it up as soon as possible. After all, it's Thanksgiving."

"You think Haley's going to find a killer in one day? He's still looking for Sterling's. It may be the same one."

"Why would someone kill an old man and a young woman?" Letty asked.

"That's what I intend to find out."

"You? Why you? I thought you were going to collect your Thanksgiving dinner and then leave town."

"I'm not leaving until I find out who's behind these two deaths."

"But why?"

"First of all, I don't like backshooters," he said. "And second, I happened to like that girl, Millie."

"Is that why you didn't come back last night?" Letty asked. "You were with her?"

"I wasn't with her last night," he said. "If I was, she'd probably still be alive."

"So you feel responsible?"

"I'm going to find the murderer," he said. "No matter who it is."

"Well," she said, "I'm glad to hear you say that. It means you'll be around a bit longer. We can . . . get together again, maybe tonight?"

"I'm going to be a little too busy for that, Letty."

"That's a shame," she said. "But maybe you'll wrap it up quickly. Do you have anyone in mind?"

"I have a few," he said.

"Want to give me a hint?"

"I don't think so," he said. "I'm going to keep it to myself until I can prove it."

"I don't know why you think the two are related," she said, "but I won't try to stop you. It can only be good for the town to solve these killings. But if I was you, I'd take a close look at Kathleen Sterling."

He decided to try and shake Letty's confidence.

123

"That's funny," he said. "She said the same thing about you."

"Me?" Letty laughed. "Why would I kill that old man?"

"Seems he was thinking of running for office against you."

She laughed again.

"He never would've beaten me."

"The word I hear around town is that you're pretty ruthless, Letty."

"You can't believe I'm ruthless enough to commit murder," she said. "I thought we . . . had something."

"Right now," he said, "everybody is under suspicion, even you."

"Then I'm especially anxious for you, Haley, or anyone else to clear this all up."

"And that's what I intend to do," he said. "I came here to let you know that."

"I guess that means we won't be having Thanksgiving dinner together."

"I'm afraid my Thanksgiving is postponed until this is all over."

"Then I think you better get to it." She placed her hands on her desk. "I have my own work to do."

"I'll leave you to it, then," he replied. "Just remember what I said."

He turned and left.

***

Mayor Miller gave Clint time to get away from City Hall before she left by the back door. She made her way to the rear of the South of Deadwood Saloon. She knocked on the door, and it was opened by Art Kittredge.

"What're you doing here?" he demanded. "Adams was just here."

"Let me in, damn it!" she barked.

He allowed her to enter, looked out the door, and then closed it.

"He just left my office," she said, turning to him. "Did he tell you what he told me?"

"He accused me of having something to do with Millie's death," Kittredge said. "Then told me he was going to find out who was behind it, and if I was guilty, he was coming for me."

"He told me about the same thing," she said. "He's not leaving town until he finds out."

"I told you it wasn't a good idea to get him involved," Kittredge said.

"I thought he'd leave town and take the blame with him," Letty said. "Then nobody would suspect us."

"So what are we going to do?"

"I think you know what we have to do," she told him.

"That'll take a lot of men, Letty."

"Well," she said, "luckily, I have a lot of men standing by."

"We're going to have to pay them," he complained.

"We'll split it," she said. "Don't worry, it'll be worth the price. Now pour me a drink and let's figure this out."

"It's Thanksgiving damn it!" he grumbled.

"And we're going to have a lot to be thankful for," she said.

Chapter Twenty-Nine

Clint walked to his hotel, but instead of going in, he sat in a chair out front, where everyone would be able to see him. He wanted it known that he was still in town. The word would probably get around that he wouldn't be leaving until he found the killer or killers of Sterling and Millie. And if the word did get around, he would know it came from Kittredge or Mayor Miller.

He wondered if the saloon owner and the mayor would get together and compare notes? And what about Kathleen Sterling? She was sure to go to Kittredge about Clint's visit.

The street in front of the hotel was almost empty. The holiday was probably keeping people indoors, preparing their big meal. Clint had been looking forward to a Thanksgiving feast, but now it seemed he would have to wait until next year for that. This Thanksgiving was all about murder, and once again he had gotten himself involved in other people's business. If he hadn't met Letty Miller and bedded her, he wouldn't be in this mess. He was going to have to start being more careful when he chose his bed partners. In point of fact, he had gladly allowed Letty Miller to seduce him. She had probably had him picked as a patsy all along. Well, she was going to find out what a mistake that was.

Now that he had talked with Kathleen Sterling, Art Kittredge and Mayor Miller, he didn't have anyone else to talk to. He wasn't going to get any help from Sheriff Haley, as he had successfully alienated the man. For all he knew, the four people he had confronted were all working together.

But he had talked with one other person in town, somebody who might have some insight into what was going on. Normally, he would have questioned the South of Deadwood bartender, but he had done that before talking with Kittredge, and had probably gotten all he was going to get from the man. That left only one other person.

He left his chair and started walking down the almost deserted street . . .

***

When he got to the café, it was empty. The man he wanted to talk with was sitting in a chair, looking bored.

"Business is slow, huh?" he asked the waiter.

"People are home, gettin' their Thanksgivin' meals ready," he said.

"What about your cook?"

"He's in the kitchen, preparin'," the waiter said. "We usually get some people in here before closing, people with no families, or cowhands whose bosses don't feed 'em on holidays. What about you?"

"I've got something else to keep me busy today," Clint said.

"The dead girl? You seemed real upset this mornin'. Didn't even have breakfast."

"Yeah, the girl."

"You want somethin' to eat now? On the house?"

"Sure, why not," Clint said. "And maybe you'll sit with me and talk."

The waiter shrugged and said, "I got nothin' else to do. Let me tell the cook to make you somethin', and I'll be back with coffee."

Clint sat to wait. This was going to work out better than he thought. If he could keep the waiter relaxed and talking, he might find some things out.

The waiter came back with a pot of coffee and two cups.

"The food'll be out soon," he said, and then sat opposite Clint.

"You know, I don't even know your name," Clint said.

"They call me Slim," the man said. "Called me that since I was a kid."

"How old are you now?"

"I'm thirty-five," Slim said. "Yeah, I know, I look older. It's 'cause I'm losin' my hair." He touched the thinning hair on his head.

"How long have you lived in Belle Fourche, Slim?"

"All my life," Slim said. "Born here, grew up here, I've worked in this little café for over fifteen years. I ain't never been nowhere else."

"I'll bet you've met a lot of people, working here."

"Oh, that's for sure," Slim said. "Folks gotta eat."

"You probably know everybody in town."

"That's for sure."

"Did you know Millie?"

"I did," Slim said. "I been in the South of Deadwood a time or two. She was a nice kid."

"What about Arthur Kittredge? Has he ever eaten here?"

"Once or twice, until bigger places opened up."

"How long's he been here?"

" 'bout ten years or so."

"You know much about him?"

Slim looked around the empty café, then back at Clint.

"You lookin' for gossip?" he asked.

"I've got to talk about something while I eat," Clint said.

"Lemme get your food and I'll tell ya a few things."

Slim ran back to the kitchen, and Clint thought he had played this just right.

Chapter Thirty

Slim came back with a heaping plate of bacon-and-eggs-and potatoes, then sat back down.

"Art Kittredge loves married women," he said, as if it was a big pronouncement.

"Oh, I've heard that."

"Did you hear about him and Walt Sterling's wife?"

"I did, yeah," Clint said. "I talked to her, and she said she hardly knew him."

"Oh, she knows him real well," Slim said. "She uses that back door to his office regularly. But then, a lot of women do." He leaned in and lowered his voice. "Including the lady mayor."

That surprised Clint, but he knew it shouldn't have.

"But she's not married."

"Don't matter," Slim said. "She's the mayor, and she gets what she wants."

"And she wants Kittredge?"

"I think she wants what he can do for her," Slim said.

"Like what?"

"Well," Slim said, "sometimes she needs men to do dirty work for her."

"Like killing?"

"I don't know about that, but sometimes the men'll come in here to eat, and they're a rough bunch."

"Rough enough to kill?"

"If they get paid enough, sure," Slim said.

"But you don't know if the mayor paid them for that."

"I don't know nothin' for sure," Slim said. "Remember, we're just gossipin'."

"Well, I'll tell you, Slim," Clint said. "I need a little more than gossip."

"Huh? Whataya mean?"

"I mean I'm going to find out who killed Sterling, and who killed Millie."

"But you ain't no lawman."

"The sheriff here isn't doing much," Clint said, "so somebody has to. Besides, I really liked Millie, and I think she was on her way to see me when she was killed."

"And you think you know who did it?"

"Not who actually did it," Clint said, "but maybe who had it done."

Slim's eyes went wide.

"The mayor?"

"Or Kittredge," Clint said. "Or maybe both. Were any of those rough types in here eating in the past few days."

"Well," Slim said, "maybe one or two. Ya know, Mr. Adams, maybe I oughtta stop talkin'. I could get in a lot of trouble. Besides which, there's others in town who could tell you more."

"Is that right?" Clint asked. "Like who?"

***

Clint figured he had gotten all he could get out of Slim, but the waiter had given him a couple of other names. So he finished his breakfast, thanked Slim, and left the café.

Slim told him how to find the two people—one was a man, one a woman. Slim said both had lived in Belle Fourche for over thirty years. They knew everyone and everything.

The woman's name was Belle, and some said the town was named after her. But Slim said the town was founded before Belle appeared.

She was an old woman who lived in a shack outside of town. Slim told Clint to be careful, she didn't like visitors. Clint followed Slim's directions and found the shack. It looked like a good stiff breeze would take it down.

"Stop right there," a voice called out, as he approached.

"Is that Belle?"

"Whataya want?"

"My name's Clint Adams," he replied. "I need to talk with you."

"About what?"

"About . . . well, everything," Clint said. "I'm trying to find out who killed Walter Sterling and a girl named Millie.

There was no immediate reply, but before he could speak again, she called out, "You're the one they call the Gunsmith, right?"

"That's right."

"Well . . . come ahead."

Clint continued on until he stood outside the front door.

"Come on in," she called.

He opened the door, found it surprisingly solid. As he entered, he sensed, too, the walls were more solid on the inside than they appeared on the outside.

He saw a wizened old woman sitting in a rocking chair in the center of the modest interior.

"This is a small place," he said.

"It's enough for me," she said. "I knew Walt Sterling. I heard he got killed while he was out hunting, the old fool. Somebody mistook him for a turkey?"

"He was shot in the back," Clint said. "Somebody killed him and tried to hide the body. I found it."

She hesitated, then said, "There's a jug over there in the corner. Bring it here. We'll have a drink and talk."

Chapter Thirty-One

Clint walked across the room, picked up the jug and carried it to Belle. He grabbed a nearby rickety chair and sat across from her. She raised the jug to her lips and took a healthy swallow, then held it out to him.

"Drink," she said.

"It's a little early—" he started, but she cut him off.

"I don't trust a man who don't take a drink," she snapped. "And I don't talk to a man I don't trust."

Clint accepted the jug and raised it to his lips. He knew a sip wouldn't satisfy her, so he took a long drink. He handed the jug back, managing not to choke as the liquor burned its way down.

Belle took another healthy drink, then set the jug down on the floor at her feet.

"Because you're tryin' to find out who killed Walt Sterling, I'll talk to you," she told him. "What do you want to know?"

"I suspect a few people of being involved," Clint said. "But I want to know if Sterling had any other enemies in town."

"Who do you suspect?"

"Art Kittredge, the mayor, and Kathleen Sterling. Two or all of them."

"Walt was a fool to marry one so young," Belle said. "Is she one of your suspects?"

"Yes, as well as Arthur Kittredge and the mayor."

Belle turned her head and spit.

"That mayor is a bitch!" she snapped. And Kittredge's a bastard. If they did it, I hope you make them pay."

"I'm assuming you knew Walt Sterling?"

"I knew him real well," she said, grinning, "if ya know what I mean. You may not believe it, but there was a time I looked as good as any saloon girl."

"I believe it," he said.

"Liar!" she said, good naturedly. "You wanna know if Walt Sterling had enemies. You ask that because he was a politician?"

"I ask because I didn't know the man," Clint said. "I've only been in town three days."

"How'd you get yerself involved in this?"

"I met the mayor, and she asked me to officiate her turkey shoot."

"You said yes because she gave ya a poke, huh?"

"Well—"

"That's okay," she said, waving a hand, "I can see how you'd give in to her. But now you know better, huh?"

"I think I do," he said. "There was also a young saloon girl killed."

"And you think the two killin's are connected?"

"I do."

"Well, I'd sure look at the young wife if I was you. And if the mayor's involved, ya gotta look at Kittredge. He might like married women, but that mayor's got him wrapped around her little finger."

"No other enemies?"

"Walt may have been a politician, but folks loved 'im. He didn't have an enemy in town until he brought that young wife here, and that Miller woman became mayor. Once he started talkin' about runnin' again, she wanted him gone. I think she came up with that turkey shoot to just get rid of him."

"Who do you think did the actual shooting?"

"That I can't tell ya," Belle said. "The mayor and Kittredge've got a tough bunch doin' their dirty work. One'a them, for sure."

She reached down for the jug, took another swig, and didn't offer it to Clint again, before setting it back down.

"What else kin I tell ya?" she asked.

"I'm told you know everyone in town."

"Pretty near," she said. "Some new folks have moved here, but I know most of the old ones."

"I was given another name of someone I could talk to," Clint said. "Festus Dillon."

She cackled at that.

"Festus has lived here pretty near as long as I have," she said. "He'll tell ya the same thing, but yeah, go ahead and talk ta him. Ya might get somethin' else."

"Then I'll ask you one more thing and leave you be," he said.

"Go ahead."

"If the mayor and Kittredge have got a bunch of guns, I could use somebody to watch my back. Do you know anybody who liked Sterling enough to do that for me?"

"Sure," Belle said. "You're already goin' ta see him."

"Festus?" he asked.

"Damn right," she said "He's an old coot, but he can still shoot straight. And nobody would suspect you was usin' him for that."

"Suits me, as long as he can do the job," Clint said. "I was told by a waiter I could find him at the Prospect Hotel."

"You sure can," she said. "That's the oldest hotel in town, and it suits 'im."

He stood up.

"I appreciate you talking to me, Belle."

"You find the yahoos who killed Walt, and you make 'em pay."

"That's what I plan to do."

Chapter Thirty-Two

Art Kittredge looked at the seven men he had gathered in a back room of his hotel. One of them was a gunman named Noah Black. It was Black who had brought the other six men in.

"This ain't my idea of how to spend Thanksgivin'," Black said.

"You're going to be paid well," Kittredge told him.

Black knew that some of the money would be coming from the mayor's pocket, but none of the other men knew that.

"Paid well for what?" he asked.

"You heard the Gunsmith's in town?"

"He had somethin' to do with that ridiculous turkey shoot, didn't he?"

"He did."

"He must be hard up for work," Black said. "Poor old fella is probably past it."

"Well," Kittredge said, "that's what I want you and your boys to prove."

Black smiled.

"That's what I was hopin' you'd say."

***

Clint left Belle's shack and made his way back to town. He found the hotel he wanted in an older section of town. It needed a paint job and a lot of boards replaced, and the sign with the name was hanging at an angle. He mounted the front porch, avoided some missing boards there, and entered the lobby. A sleepy-eyed, elderly desk clerk watched him as he approached.

"We ain't got no rooms," he said, when Clint reached the desk.

"You're kidding," Clint said. "You're filled up?"

"Nope," the clerk said, "we just ain't got no clean rooms."

"Then it's a good thing I'm not looking for a room," Clint commented.

"What're ya lookin' for, then?"

"Festus Dillon."

"Oh yeah, he's here," the clerk said. "You'll find him in the honeymoon suite." The clerk laughed.

"And where would that be?"

"Upstairs, room ten," the clerk said.

"I hope I won't be interrupting something," Clint said.

"I doubt it," the clerk said. "You'll probably just wake 'im up."

"I'll do my best."

Clint went up the stairs, again avoiding missing and loose boards, found room ten and knocked on the door. He heard mattress springs, then footsteps, and finally the door opened. A small, bandy-legged man looked at him from behind a face full of black and grey whiskers.

"Yer the Gunsmith," he said.

"That's right," Clint said. "How'd you know that?"

"I heard you was in town, and I know everybody else," the man said. "Whataya want with me?"

"I came to see you because you know everybody in town."

"Who sent ya?"

"Belle." Clint didn't know her last name.

"Ole Belle sent ya?" Festus asked. "Well, come on in then."

Clint entered and closed the door behind him.

Festus pulled up his hanging suspenders, then turned to look at Clint.

"How is the ol' girl?"

"She's pretty good."

"She make you pull from her jug?"

"She sure did."

The little man laughed. Clint noticed a Winchester that had seen better days leaning against the wall in a corner.

"I got nothin' to offer you to drink."

"That's okay," Clint said. "What I got from Belle's jug is still burning its way down.

Festus laughed again and asked, "What kin I do for ya?"

"I heard you knew Walt Sterling."

"I did," Festus said. "That ol' fella was a damn good mayor. But he was a damn fool for marryin' that young gal." He pointed at Clint. "Wait, you found his body."

"I did," Clint said, "and now I'm trying to find out who killed him."

"Well, good for you," Festus said. "Whoever did it should be strung up. Who ya think done it? The wife? The mayor?"

"Why the mayor?"

" 'cause she wantsta stay mayor."

"What about Art Kittredge?" Clint asked.

"If the mayor had it done, then he helped her," Festus said.

"That's what I think," Clint said, "but I'm told those two have a lot of tough nuts working for them."

"They got a fella named Noah Black does their dirty work," Festus said, "and he's got some toughs workin' fer him."

"Well, I guess I'm going to be going up against some of those guns," Clint said. "I told Belle I needed somebody to watch my back, and she suggested you."

Chapter Thirty-Three

"I'm sixty-five years old," Festus said.

Clint looked over at the rifle, which looked about the same age.

"So?"

"If that don't bother you," Festus said, "I'll be proud to watch your back."

Clint didn't have too many other choices.

"Can I look at your rifle?"

"Gracie?" Festus said. "Sure."

He walked to the corner to get the rifle and carry it to Clint. Clint looked it over, hefted it, sighted down the barrel—which he thought would be bent, but wasn't.

"It could use a cleaning," Clint said, handing it back.

Festus laughed and said, "So could I, but we'll both get the job done."

"Okay, then," Clint said. "When I'm on the street, I need you to make sure I don't get shot in the back."

"Like Walt Sterling," Festus said. "Got it."

"How well did you know Sterling?" Clint asked.

"A lot of years ago I worked for him," Festus said. "Then we both got to the age where people stopped thinkin' we could do the job."

"If people thought that, why would Mayor Miller think he might beat her in the next election?"

"People hate her more than they doubted him," Festus said. "He woulda beat her, easy."

"But would she have killed him for that reason?"

"She wants what she wants," Festus said, "and she'll do whatever she has to do to get it."

"That's what people keep telling me."

"So where do we start?"

"Festus," Clint said, "I don't see much time for a Thanksgiving dinner in our immediate future."

"I ain't had a family, or a Thanksgivin' for a lotta years, Mr. Adams."

"If you're going to be watching my back, I think you can call me Clint."

"Okay, Clint."

Clint looked down at the man's toes sticking out from holes in his socks.

"Maybe we better start with you putting on your boots . . ."

***

"I don't like this," Sheriff Haley said. "Blaming the Gunsmith for a killing, sure, but killing him here in town?" He shook his head.

He was in Art Kittredge's office with the saloon owner and Mayor Miller.

"You agreed to go along with this, Haley," Letty said.

"Yeah, I did," Haley said, "but that was before we were talking about three murders,"

"You knew we were going to kill the old man," Kittredge said.

"We needed him out of the way to help the town grow," Letty said.

"I know, I know," Haley said, "but why did Millie have to die? What did that poor kid do?"

"We didn't know how much she heard, or what she was going to tell Adams," Kittredge said.

"And now you want to kill the Gunsmith," Haley said. "That's really gonna put Belle Fourche on the map for the wrong reason."

"The reason doesn't matter, as long as we're on the map," Letty said. "Just think of it. The Gunsmith killed so close to the town where Wild Bill Hickok was killed. We're going to be part of a legend."

"And all you have to do is stay out of the way," Kittredge said. "Go and find a place to have Thanksgiving dinner and stay off the street."

"You can do that, Sheriff, can't you?" Letty asked.

"The town is still gonna want to know who killed Walt Sterling."

"We'll take care of that," Letty said.

"Just get out of here and do your job," Kittredge said.

"And by that we mean . . . don't! Go to the bar and have a drink or two."

The lawman turned and slunk from the room.

Kittredge and Letty turned to face each other.

"This can still work," Letty told him. "We can get rid of Adams and Kathleen all at once."

"How do you figure?" Kittredge asked.

"Black and his men get rid of Adams," Letty said, "and we let it be known that she paid him to kill Sterling." She shrugged. "Simple."

"Yeah, simple," Kittredge said. "All we've got to do is kill The Gunsmith."

"Noah and his men will see to that," she assured him. "They're being paid enough."

***

They agreed not to be seen together, so Clint left the hotel first. At that point, he didn't see or feel anyone's eyes on him.

With the streets mostly empty for Thanksgiving, it was going to be hard for Noah Black and his men to try and follow Clint. It was more likely they would simply lie in wait for him, on a corner, from an alley or a second story window.

Festus came out after Clint, gave him a good head start, and then followed. The old man still had sharp eyes, and he swept both sides of the street. When they got onto Main Street, he was really going to have to stay alert.

Chapter Thirty-Four

Clint had never heard of Noah Black, but he knew the type. He would be a man who made his living with a gun, was probably good with it, but needed to surround himself with guns to back his play. Those gun hands would be less steady, but for sale.

Clint felt the need for a drink but didn't want to get it at the South of Deadwood, so he walked until he found another saloon. This one was smaller and called The Last Stand Saloon. As he entered, he hoped the name wouldn't be prophetic.

The place was small and empty, except for one man seated at a table with his head face down. There was a half-empty mug of beer next to him.

There was a small bar with a meager collection of bottles on the wall behind it, and a tall, thin bartender.

"Happy Thanksgivin'," the man said. "What'll ya have?"

"A beer."

"Comin' up."

The man put the mug on the bar. Clint sipped, found it remarkably cold and good, considering the place.

"You going to be serving for Thanksgiving?" Clint asked.

"Whiskey and beer for anyone who comes in," the man said. "I got no family to worry about."

"And him?" Clint inclined his head toward the man at the table.

"He's a regular," the bartender said. "He's got no family either."

"So no Thanksgiving dinner for you?"

"I got some beef jerky and beans waitin' for me when I close up. What about you?"

"No dinner for me either," Clint said.

"Wait a minute," the man said. "You're Adams, ain'tcha?"

"That's right."

Clint looked over at the man at the table. It didn't seem likely he would be one of Noah Black's men, but he kept an eye on him anyway.

"Ain't you been doin' your drinkin' at the South of Deadwood?"

"I thought I'd make a change," Clint said. "That okay with you?"

"Hey," the man said, with a shrug, "wherever you wanna wet your whistle is okay with me. They say you found old Mayor Sterling's body."

"I did."

"That old guy was okay," the bartender said. "A shame somebody killed him right before Thanksgiving. He's got a helluva cook in his house."

"I think his wife is still having dinner made."

"What a crazy thing to do, bringin' her back to town after marryin' her."

"He married her out of town?"

"He went to Denver on business and came back with a young wife. Nobody could believe it."

"How long have they been married?"

"A few months is all. Poor old sod. I hope she kept him happy for those few months."

"I've heard people saying they thought she had him killed," Clint said. "What do you think of that?"

"I don't see why she would," the man said. "Seems to me she coulda killed him between the sheets. Then she woulda inherited everything."

"Well, she gets it all, anyway," Clint said.

"I guess so. You ain't been in town that long, but who do you think killed him?"

"I don't know," Clint said, "but I'm working on finding out."

"Better you than the sheriff," the man said. "He's useless."

"I heard that, too." Clint finished his beer. The man with his head on the table still hadn't moved. "You sure he's alive?"

"He lifts his head every once in a while to take a drink," the bartender said. "I keep his glass full."

"Well," Clint said, tossing a coin on the bar, "Happy Thanksgiving. Enjoy your jerky and beans."

"I intend to."

Clint turned and left the small saloon. The only person he saw on the street was Festus, leaning against a building and watching. The old man probably could have used a drink.

Festus saw Clint looking at him, rubbed his nose and nodded. Clint took that to mean the street was clean. Nobody getting ready to shoot him in the back—yet.

Clint may have had some experience with this sort of thing, solving murders, but he still didn't consider himself to be a detective. His friend, Talbot Roper, would have had a plan about what to do next, but Clint didn't. He sniffed the air and thought he could smell turkey cooking. The aroma was probably coming from a variety of homes. He wondered what Kathleen Sterling would do if he actually did show up at her house for turkey dinner? It would probably throw her completely off balance, or she would be confident enough to handle it. A beautiful woman like that was used to handling men. He wondered how well she handled Art Kittredge, or if it was the other way around?

Chapter Thirty-Five

Letty Miller looked at Art Kittredge who was lying on the other side of her bed. They were both naked, and sweaty from their exertions.

"So, what're you going to do about your little widow?" she asked.

"Hey, she's a beautiful girl," Kittredge said. "What do you think I'm going to do about her?"

"But she's not married anymore," Letty said. she leaned over and ran her finger down his chest to his belly and then to his now limp cock. "You like married women."

"Then what am I doin' here with you?" he asked, watching her hand as it closed around him.

"You know there's no danger of me wanting to marry you," she said, tightening her hold. "I just want to fuck you."

"And you want me to back your plays with money, if need be," he added.

"Well, yes." she said. "But for now, this will do." She leaned over and took his semi-hard cock in her mouth, suckled him until he was fully hard, then released him, climbed into his lap, took him into her pussy and rode him that way until he exploded inside of her.

As she climbed off him, she asked, "You going to Thanksgiving dinner at her house tonight?"

Breathlessly, he said, "I don't know. Maybe."

"Well, if you do, see if she can ride you the way I just did."

"I've been to bed with her," Kittredge said. "She may be a beauty, but she's nothing like you, Letty."

"Nobody is," she said, "and you better remember that."

He got up and started dressing.

"Are you going to sleep with your friend Adams again?" he asked.

"I'd like to," she said, "at least one more time, but I don't think I'm going to be able to."

"You mean he can resist you?" Kittredge asked.

"I mean," she said, "he's going to be dead."

***

Wearing a robe draped over her naked form, she walked Kittredge to the front door.

"What are you going to be doing the rest of the day?" he asked.

"I'll be right here in my kitchen, making a turkey dinner. If you feel like it, stop by and I'll feed you. That is, if you can resist your little friend."

"My little friend is worth a lot of money, Letty," Kittredge said. "It'd make a nice big war chest for your political future."

"Why Arthur," she said, "I didn't know you cared."

She pressed up against him and kissed him. He could feel every curve of her naked body and its heat right through the robe.

"This'll be over soon, Letty," he said. "No more Kathy and no more Clint Adams. Just us and what we want."

As Kittredge went out the door, she closed it behind him and said, "Wrong, Arthur, it'll be me and what I want. Happy Thanksgiving."

***

The only thing Clint could think to do was sit in a chair in front of the hotel, wait and see what happened. It certainly wasn't his idea of the way he was going to spend Thanksgiving. Sitting in that chair, the whole town seemed to smell like cooking turkey.

Festus had taken up a position across the street, in the doorway of the hardware store, which was locked up tight for the holiday.

***

Midday, Thanksgiving Day, nothing had happened, yet. Eventually, Clint heard the sound of approaching horses, and then a group of riders came down Main Street. Maybe this was Noah Black and his men.

As they got closer, he stood up and watched them from the hotel porch. Festus had also come to attention in the doorway, ready for anything.

The riders were strung out behind one man, who seemed to be the leader. He looked older than Clint would have thought. The man saw him and changed direction, his men following him. As they got closer, Clint could see the man in front was in his sixties.

Festus came running across the street, calling out, "Don't shoot, Clint, don't shoot!" He reached the porch just as the riders did. "These ain't gunmen. This is Mr. Chantry and his boys from the Bar-C ranch. It's one of the biggest spreads in the county."

"Are you Clint Adams?" Chantry asked.

"I am."

"Then I think we oughtta talk."

"Step down," Clint said, "and let's do it."

Chapter Thirty-Six

Chantry suggested they go to the South of Deadwood to talk, but Clint said he preferred someplace smaller and took the men to the Last Stand Saloon. The bartender was surprised to see so many customers come into the place. There was still only one table taken by the same man with his head on the table.

"Get some drinks at the bar, boys," Chantry told his men. "I'm gonna sit at a table with this feller."

"Right, boss," one of them said and led the others to the bar.

"Let's sit over there, Adams," Chantry said, leading the way to a table across the room away from the bar and the sleeping man.

Clint and Chantry sat, and one of the rancher's men brought beers over for them.

"Thanks, Jim," Chantry said. "That's my foreman."

Clint and the foreman nodded at each other, and the man went back to the bar.

"What brings you to town, Mr. Chantry?" Clint asked. "Especially on Thanksgiving Day."

"There was a time when Walt Sterling and me was friends," Chantry said. "He was the mayor, and I was buildin' my place up."

"I've been looking into Sterling's death, trying to find his friends and his enemies. How come nobody's said a word about you?"

"Because I said we once were friends," Chantry said. "We hadn't been for years."

"Why?"

"Let's just say we had a falling out."

"When?"

"Oh, maybe thirty years ago." Chantry drank from his beer.

"What was it about?" Clint asked.

Chantry put his beer down.

"Who remembers?"

"Then why are you here in town and not celebrating Thanksgiving on your ranch?"

Chantry laughed.

"My wife asked me the same question," he said. "Walt and I may not have been friends for years, but that doesn't mean somebody should've killed him. I want to know who did it, and why?"

"That's what I'm trying to find out."

"Well then," Chantry said, "me and my men are at your service. Use us any way you see fit."

"What about Thanksgiving and your wife?"

"I promised her I'd be back tonight."

"If you think we'll find the killer by then—"

"We have to find him, or her, by then," he said. "I promised my wife I'd be back for Thanksgiving dinner."

"Mr. Chantry—"

"Come on, man!" Chantry snapped. "You must have some idea who did it."

"A saloon girl was also killed," Clint said.

"What's that got to do with Walt's death?"

"They thought she was on her way to tell me something," Clint said. "In fact, she had already told me the night before that Kittredge and Mrs. Sterling were planning something."

"So you think they killed her to shut her up."

"Yes."

"Then why haven't you done something?"

"Like what?"

"You're the Gunsmith," Chantry said. "Kill 'em."

"I don't kill people in cold blood, Mr. Chantry."

"I'll pay you."

"I sure as hell don't kill for money."

"Then why do you have this ridiculous reputation as a cold-blooded killer?" Chantry asked.

"Newspapers, and dime novels," Clint said. "It's all exaggeration."

"Then what are you, Mr. Gunsmith?"

"I'm fast and accurate with a gun," Clint said, "and when I need to, I use my gun to make a point."

"And do you intend to do that here?"

"Once I'm sure I know who I'm dealing with, yes," Clint said. "I also think the mayor's involved."

"That woman?"

"You know her?"

"I quit the Town Council when she took office," Chantry said. "I wouldn't deal with her. You think she had Walt killed?"

"There's a good chance."

"But why?"

"She didn't want him to run against her."

"He was gonna run again?"

"He was talking about it."

"That old fool!"

"Wasn't he a good mayor?"

"When he was younger, yes," Chantry said. "But he was at an age when he couldn't have handled the stress."

"Well, there was no guarantee that he was going to run, but she might not have wanted to chance it."

"So you're telling me two women and a saloon owner killed him?"

"That's the way it looks," Clint told him, "but I can't prove it."

"So why doesn't the sheriff do something?" the rancher asked.

"He's under the mayor's thumb."

"Any man she deals with is under her thumb," Chantry said. "That was why I quit the council" He finished his beer and set the empty mug down on the table. "How did you get involved anyway?"

"I'm afraid I was under her thumb for a short time," Clint admitted, "until I started to learn what the woman was really like."

"Do these people know you suspect them?"

"Yes."

"How?"

"I told them."

"Are you mad?" Chantry asked. "They'll probably try to kill you."

"I figured that."

The rancher sat back and looked at Clint with renewed respect.

Chapter Thirty-Seven

"You want them to come after you," he said. "Then you can use your gun."

"It would seem the only way."

"They won't come for you themselves, you know. They'll use hired guns," Chantry said.

"There are some already in town."

"You'll need my men to back you."

"If I have your men around me, they'll never try," Clint said. "I've got someone watching my back."

A grim look came over the rancher's face.

"I heard Walt was shot in the back."

"He was," Clint said. "That's the main reason I'm still here. I lost a good friend that way."

Chantry hazarded a guess.

"Hickok?"

"Yes. If I'd been in Deadwood, Bill might not have been killed."

"So you want to solve this murder."

"Yes. I want the backshooter and whoever put him up to it. Also, whoever killed that poor young saloon girl, when all she was trying to do was help me."

"You're taking a big chance."

"I know it," Clint said.

"At least let me leave you a man or two."

"You see how empty the streets are for the holiday," Clint said. "You leave me any men and they'll stand out. You and your people go home and have Thanksgiving. I'll take care of this."

Chantry stared at Clint, then said, "My wife's gonna like you. If you get this finished in time, come to the ranch for Thanksgiving dinner."

"Thanks for the invitation, but I don't really feel I'm going to have anything to be thankful for by the time this is done."

"I don't blame you," Chantry said. "You're gonna have to do some killing."

"Yes."

Chantry stood up and extended his hand. Clint stood and took it.

"I'm glad to have met you, Adams," he said. "I'm sorry I believed all that stuff about you. You're an honorable man."

"Thank you, Mr. Chantry."

Chantry turned and headed for the door, calling out, "Come on, boys! We're headin' home for Thanksgiving."

His men cheered and followed him out.

Festus came to Clint's table, carrying a beer in one hand and Gracie in the other.

"Sit down, Festus," Clint said.

The old man did, setting his rifle on the table.

"Did he offer to help?" he asked.

"Yup."

"And you said no?"

"Yup."

"Why'd ya do that?"

"Because with him and his men around, I don't think anybody would try for me."

"And you want them to?"

"They're going to do it, eventually," Clint said. "It's the only way to get rid of me, since I'm not leaving on my own. So, it might as well happen in my time, not theirs. If that bothers you, I'll understand."

"Naw, I'm still in," Festus said. "Like you said, they're gonna try for you. They won't even see me comin'." The old man cackled and drank his beer. "So when do we go back on the street?"

"After another beer," Clint said, "Come on."

He led the way to the bar, walking past the man with his head on the table.

"Two more beers," he told the barkeep.

"Thanks for all the business." The man said, setting the beers down. "Best Thanksgivin' I've had in a while. This one's on me."

"Thanks," Clint said.

He and Festus drank their beers and set the empty mugs down.

"There's gonna be a ruckus, ain't there?" the bartender asked.

"There is, indeed," Clint said.

"Well, good luck."

Clint and Festus headed for the door.

***

Noah Black was on a rooftop, across from the Last Stand. He had seen Chantry and his men ride in. At first he thought the rancher and his men might have ridden in to offer help to the Gunsmith, which would have made it necessary to change his plans. But the men soon rode out of town, so there was no reason to change.

He left the roof to put the plan into action.

***

Mayor Letty Miller looked out her office window at the all but deserted Main Street. She would soon be going home to prepare her Thanksgiving dinner. She wanted to be so involved when Black and his men made their move on Clint Adams.

She was sorry Clint had taken Walt Sterling's death so personal. Her intention had been to sleep with him again, after which he would leave town, the blame for Sterling's death following him. Once the girl, Millie, was killed, that confirmed that the Gunsmith would have to be handled in town.

The death of Clint Adams in Belle Fourche on Thanksgiving Day would be legendary.

***

Arthur Kittredge sat in his office, a glass of brandy on the desk in front of him. He knew two women in town wanted his presence at their Thanksgiving dinner, but he wasn't concerned with either. He was more interested in what would happen when Noah Black and his men moved on Clint Adams. Standing alone against Black and his crew, he certainly had no chance. Black thought the Gunsmith was past his best days, and so would succumb to his planned attack.

Kittredge hoped that was true.

Chapter Thirty-Eight

Noah Black had six men. Four were useful—he didn't even care what their names were—but two were very talented with their side arms and rifles. They were Beckett and Cartwright. He met with those two in the small back room of the South of Deadwood Saloon, which was closed for Thanksgiving.

"I'm sendin' the others after Adams first," he said. "The outcome will let us know how much he's lost over the years."

"It doesn't matter," Beckett said. "We can take him."

"That's right," Cartwright said. "We been waitin' for a chance like this."

Both men were in their late twenties. Black, who was forty, thought that, though talented, they were foolish.

"I need the two of you to stop thinkin', and just act," he instructed. "You need to do this as I say, understand?"

Both hesitated, but then Beckett said, "Yes, we understand."

"If the others take him, it's just as well and we'll all get paid," Black explained. "If they don't, then you two will get that chance you've been waitin' for."

Both men nodded.

"Then here's what I want you to do . . .

***

Festus continued to shadow Clint as he walked around Belle Fourche. In all his years living there he had never seen the streets this deserted, even on holidays. It was as if everyone knew there was trouble brewing and was staying inside.

He thought Clint Adams was probably crazy, walking around the deserted town, making a target out of himself. He kept his rifle, Gracie, ready, just in case.

In the early evening Festus was getting tired of following Clint around. Suddenly, he heard someone behind him. He turned and saw a single man, in his thirties, carrying a rifle and looking past him.

As he came abreast of the old man he said, "You better get off the street, old timer. It's gonna get rough."

Festus let the man walk past, and it was obvious he was creeping up on Clint. It looked like something was finally going to happen.

There had to be more than just this one man. He hoped Clint was alert as he said he was . . .

***

Clint knew the man was behind Festus before the old man did. He also knew that meant there had to be more. He thought about taking on the one before the others showed their faces. Then he would be able to get some information from him. But he had no idea if this was the first move, or if this one was just a spotter, keeping Clint in view. If he moved against this one, it might bring the others out. Did he want to do that, or let them move in their own time?

He decided to take a turn down the street to the Last Stand Saloon. It was one of the few places in town that was still open. He could actually make a last stand there, if it came to that, but he had another idea.

He entered the small saloon, hoping Festus wouldn't follow him in.

***

Festus didn't know what Clint had planned, but he thought it would be better to take on one man than a bunch. Clint might have other ideas, but if he got mad, so be it. He watched the man creep closer to The Last Stand and peer in the dirty window. He came up behind him and stuck Gracie's muzzle into the man's back.

"Wha—oh, it's you," the man said, looking behind him. "I told you to get off the street."

"We're both gettin' off the street, partner." He put Gracie's muzzle in the man's face, this time. "Gimme your rifle and step inside. Let's have a drink."

"You don't know what you're doin', friend," the man said, releasing his rifle. "You're gonna get some folks real mad atcha."

"Everybody's gonna be mad at me," Festus said. "What the hell. Move!"

***

"Back already?" the bartender asked. "I was just gonna close up for dinner."

"I think your jerky and beans are going to have to wait, friend."

"My name's Tyler," the bartender said, "and what's goin' on?"

"Just get ready to duck," Clint told him.

At that point Festus came through the batwing doors with another man in front of him.

"This feller was on your tail, Clint," the old man said. "I thought maybe we'd buy him a drink and have a talk."

"You heard the man, Tyler," Clint said. "Pour the man a drink."

"Make that two, friend," Festus said.

Instead, Tyler poured three shots of whiskey.

173

"Have a drink and tell me your name, friend," Clint said.

"Bill Williams," the man said. "What's this about, friend? I was just walkin' down the street when this crazy old coot sticks his gun in my face."

"This is going to go better for you if you just answer my questions, Bill."

Williams looked at Clint, Festus, Tyler, even the man with his head on the table, then picked up his drink and knocked it back.

"Whataya wanna know?" he asked.

"When's Noah Black going to make his move?"

Williams looked surprised.

"You know about that?"

"I know everything except when he's going to make his move."

"We wuz gettin' ready to make our move," Williams said. "That's why I was comin' up behind ya."

"Out on the street?"

"Yeah, except you ducked in here."

"What was the play going to be?" Clint asked.

"We wuz gonna flank ya."

"How many of you are there?"

"Four, countin' me."

"What kind of guns do the others have?"

"One's got a rifle, like me," Williams said, "the other two have handguns."

"That's it?" Clint asked. "Four?"

"Noah's got two others, but he's holdin' them back."

"Why?"

"They're good with their guns," Williams said, "Fast. But Noah was givin' us a chance first."

"Why?"

"We all wanted a chance at the Gunsmith," Williams said.

"When was Black going to step in?"

"He wanted to see what you got left, first," Williams said. "He thinks you're old and past it. . . I mean, uh, no offense."

"Is he any good?"

"He's the fastest one of all," Williams said. "But he's smart, too."

"We'll see about that," Clint said. "Now comes the real important question."

"What's that?"

"Who's paying the freight for this play?"

"I don't know his name," Williams said, "but he runs the South of Deadwood Saloon."

"Tyler," Clint said, slapping the man on the back, "pour my friend another drink."

Chapter Thirty-Nine

"Sit over there and don't wake sleeping beauty," Clint said.

The man took his second drink with him to a table.

"One more thing, Williams," Clint said.

Williams turned.

"What's that?"

"Who killed Sterling and the girl?" Clint asked. "Who shot that old man in the back?"

"I dunno," Williams said. "I swear. That happened even before me and the others got involved."

"Okay," Clint said. "Sit."

Williams sat and downed his drink.

"What'll your three friends do when you don't come out?" Clint asked.

"I dunno," Williams said. "We wuz supposed to take care of you out in the street. I-I guess they'll wait til we come out."

"But they saw Festus bring you in here at gunpoint," Clint reminded the man. "That's going to tell them they need a new plan."

"I dunno," Williams said, again. "Noah told us not to come back unless we got you."

"Is that right," Clint said. "I guess he figured if you didn't get me, you wouldn't be coming back anyway. What do you think?"

"I guess . . ."

Clint hoped the other three men outside were at least as dumb as Bill Williams was. If they were told not to come back unless they got him, Clint figured eventually, they would be coming in.

"Tyler, is there a back door to this place?" he asked.

"Are you kiddin'? We're lucky we got a front door."

"Whatta we gonna do?" Festus asked.

"We're going to wait."

"But—what about my Thanksgiving jerky and beans?" Tyler whined.

"Where were you going to make it?" Clint asked.

"I got a kitchen in the back."

"Well then, go ahead and cook."

Tyler started away, then turned back and said, "For everybody?"

"I could eat," Festus said.

"You heard the man," Clint said. "Beans for everybody."

Chapter Forty

"Festus," Clint said, pointing, "you sit over there."

"Right."

"I'll sit here," Clint said. "When they come in, we'll have them in a crossfire."

"What about me?" Williams asked.

"What about you?"

"I'm sittin' right in the middle of the room," Williams said. "I might get hit."

"Well," Clint said, "when your friends come in, hit the deck."

Clint looked at the sleeping man. He wasn't in the center of the room. If he didn't move, he would probably be all right. And the several times Clint was in The Last Stand, the man had not moved a muscle.

Time ticked by, and Williams fidgeted nervously. Eventually, Tyler came out carrying plates of jerky and beans. He put one down on the table in front of Festus, and one on Clint's table.

"Hey," Williams said. "How about me?"

Tyler looked at Clint.

"Sure," Clint said, "I did say everybody."

Tyler went back in the kitchen, came out with two more plates. He put one down on William's table, and one on the table of the sleeping man.

"Happy Thanksgiving," Clint said to the room.

***

They finished eating and Tyler cleared away the plates, except for the sleeping man's, which was untouched.

"Leave it," Clint said. "He'll wake up eventually, right?"

"Usually," Tyler said.

They continued to sit and wait, which to Festus was better than walking around town aimlessly waiting for someone to shoot.

There was one rather grimy window to the right of the door, so Clint said to Festus, "Keep your eye on the window, and I'll watch the door. There's no other way in."

Williams continued to fidget nervously. He was ready to duck to the floor and turn the table over at a moment's notice. He wished he hadn't taken this job at all, but his best friend—who was one of the other three men outside—had gotten him involved with a promise of a good pay day.

179

The rest of the town was probably in their homes, dining on turkey and being thankful for what they had. Clint assumed that included Kathleen Sterling and Letty Miller.

He was wrong . . .

***

When a knock came at her door, Letty hoped it was either Clint Adams or Art Kittredge. She found herself hoping it was Clint Adams, wanting to have sex with her one last time—and it *would* be his last time.

But when she answered the door, clad only in her robe, she found herself looking at the beautiful face of Kathleen Sterling.

"What the hell are you doing here?" she demanded.

Kathleen stormed past her. Letty had no choice but to close the door and follow her in.

"I hope nobody saw you come here," Letty said.

"Don't worry," Kathleen said. "I was careful."

"What are you doing here?"

"That bitch said she was going to cook, but instead she just left."

"Did you really expect her to cook?"

"I wanted my turkey dinner," Kathleen said. "It was supposed to be part of my celebration."

"Well, since you're here you might as well. My turkey's almost ready."

"Are you expecting anyone else?"

"Not really," Letty said.

"Well then," Kathleen said, "before we eat let's start our celebration a different way."

She approached Letty and took hold of the front of her robe. The garment clung to Letty's solid frame, the outline of her large nipples very prominent. Kathleen pulled the robe open and peeled it down from Letty's shoulders. The mayor allowed the robe to drop to the floor, gathered at her feet. She was ready to start their celebration, as their plan was almost complete. When it was done, both men—Clint Adams and Kittredge—would be gone.

Kathleen took Letty's large breasts in her hands, leaned down and, one at a time, took a nipple into her mouth and sucked it. Letty did not make a habit of having sex with women, but Kathleen was the most beautiful girl she had ever seen, so why not?

She leaned her head back and moaned as Kathleen's mouth worked its magic on her breasts. She spent a lot of time covering both beautiful mounds of flesh with her lips and tongue. By the time Letty was wet between her legs, she pushed the young girl away and said, her voice hoarse, "Not here. Let's go upstairs."

181

"That suits me," Kathleen said.

She grabbed Letty's hand and tugged her up the stairs.

***

"How long we gonna wait?" Festus finally asked.

"They know if they go back to Black with news that they didn't get me, they'll be in trouble. They'll be coming in, eventually."

"Why don't we go out and get it over with?" Festus asked.

"As soon as we go out the door, they'll start shooting. We'll be at a disadvantage because we'll have to spot them before we can shoot back. This way, as they come in, we'll know where they are."

"What if they don't come in?" Williams asked.

"What do you think they'll do, Williams?" Clint asked.

Williams knew his friend, Dalton, usually made the wrong decision. That was why they usually let someone like Black, do the thinking.

"Oh," he said, "they'll come in."

"Then we wait."

***

When Kathleen and Letty got to the bedroom, Letty quickly grabbed the other girl and kissed her, pressing their bodies close together. Then she busied herself undoing all the buttons of Kathleen's dress and peeling it off until the girl was also naked. Letty preferred the girl's gorgeous, sleek breasts to her own, which she considered blocky. She grabbed them and covered them with kisses, while Kathleen's hands roamed her body.

"You are so damned beautiful," Letty said, huskily.

"I wish I had your tits," Kathleen said.

They continued to kiss each other's body. The only thing they really had in common was smooth and supple skin. Eventually, wrapped up in each other's arms, they fell onto the bed together.

Their hands continued to roam and soon they were fingering each other's wet pussies, filling the rooms with the sounds of their moans and groans. Letty preferred a man's nice thick cock poking into her, but this had its own advantages as well. A woman knew just where and how to touch another woman.

Kathleen began to kiss her way down Letty's body and the lady mayor decided to lie back and allow the girl to enjoy herself. The younger girl got down between her older lover's legs and dove in, covering her vagina with kisses and licks until she had Letty gushing wetly with a loud scream . . .

Chapter Forty-One

As breathless as Letty was, she felt the need to repay Kathleen for the pleasure the younger woman had just given her.

"Lie back, darling girl," she said, pressing Kathleen down to the mattress.

"Your turkey is going to burn," Kathleen warned.

"It makes the skin taste that much better," Letty said.

She ran her hands over Kathleen's smooth body, then leaned over to kiss her way down until her face was nestled between the girl's exquisite thighs. She worked on the girl with her tongue and lips until her face was covered with sweet nectar, then busied herself giving as much pleasure as she had received. Kathleen's hands closed on the sheets as her heels beat the mattress like a drum. Finally, she screamed as Letty mounted her and muffled her screams with her own mouth . . .

***

"This is delicious," Kathleen said, sometime later.

"I told you," Letty said, "a little burning makes the skin taste better."

"It's so crispy," Kathleen said. She was comfortable in a robe Letty had loaned her.

"Are you happy now that you have your Thanksgiving dinner?" Letty asked.

"Yes," she said, "but tell me, is this all going to be resolved?"

"Oh yes," she said. "Things are in motion. By midnight there will be no Clint Adams, and no Art Kittredge to worry about."

"Just us," Kathleen said, "and my husband's money."

Letty picked up her glass of wine and held it out. Kathleen did the same and they clinked glasses.

"Here's to your husband's money," Letty said, and they clinked. "In a scant six hours everything will be ours."

"Art is going to be a very disappointed man," Kathleen said.

"Art Kittredge is a pig," Letty said. "He deserves what he's going to get."

"And you're sure your man can do it?"

"Kittredge thinks Noah Black works for him," Letty said, "but Noah's never let me down."

"And you'll give him a little of what you gave me tonight?" Kathleen asked.

"It's a small price to pay," Letty assured her. "You suck a man's penis and he'll do anything you ask. They're all pigs."

"Even the Gunsmith?" Kathleen asked. "He has quite a reputation with the ladies, I hear."

"And well deserved," Letty said. "Yes, it's a shame to kill him. Every once in a while you find a good one, but he chose his own fate."

"Too bad I didn't get to try him," Kathleen said.

"At least you never had to sleep with that dried up old husband of yours."

"I had Art Kittredge to keep me occupied, but still, Clint Adams might have been fun."

"You're going to have to be happy with what you get from me, love."

"Oh," Kathleen said, "believe me, I am."

They both laughed and turned their attention back to their meal . . .

***

"We're goin' in," Sam Dalton said.

"Are you sure?" one of the other men asked. "Maybe we should go back—"

"If we go to Noah Black without Clint Adams dead, he'll have our heads."

"So how do we play this?" the other man asked.

None of the three men was used to making plans, but Dalton felt the need to step up."

"You two go through the batwing doors," he said, "and start shootin'."

"And you?"

"I'm gonna go through that dirty window," Dalton said. "Adams will never expect it."

"Why not?"

Dalton didn't really know why he had said that, so he told them, "Never mind! Just do it, and we'll get this thing over with."

"What about Williams? He's inside, he might get hit by flyin' lead."

"Bigger shares for us, then."

"I thought he was your friend," one of them said.

"He is," Dalton said, "but he was dumb enough to get taken."

"What about that old timer?"

"We do him, too," Dalton said, "and anybody else who gets in the way." He drew his gun. "You boys ready?"

Chapter Forty-Two

"Get ready," Clint said, in a low tone.

"Wha—" Festus started, but then he too heard the footsteps on the loose boards outside.

"Oh God," Williams said.

"Sit still!" Clint hissed.

Clint took his gun out of his holster and held it at the ready on the table. Festus did the same thing with Gracie.

Tyler ducked down behind the bar.

The sleeping man remained sleeping. By this time, Clint was certain the man had died.

It got very quiet outside.

Festus cocked the hammer on Gracie and pointed the rifle at the window.

Clint kept his eyes on the batwing doors. He doubted he would see legs before they burst in, but the men were not as dumb as Williams they were dumber. Clint saw their legs a split second before they crashed through the doors.

He lifted his gun and fired twice. Both men were shocked when his bullet struck them each in the chest.

The filthy window shattered as Dalton leaped through it, gun in hand. Festus pulled his trigger once and Gracie spoke. The bullet struck Dalton just below the chin. He was dead by the time it exited through the back of his head.

Williams had no time to even duck down behind a table when it was all over.

The sleeping man woke, lifted his head, pulled a gun from his belt and said, "What the hell—" then he saw the plate of food on the table. "Oh," he said, put his gun back in his belt and started to eat.

***

The South of Deadwood Saloon was close enough to the action for Kittredge, Noah Black, Beckett and Cartwright to hear the shots as they sat in the back room.

"Fools," Noah Black said.

"Wha—" Kittredge started. "It's not done?"

"Not enough shots," Black said. "Two of those shots came from a pistol, one a rifle. I sent four men. There should've been a lot more shots than that."

"Our turn?" Beckett said

"Exactly," Black said. "Get goin'."

The two men stood and left the room.

"Are they good enough?" Kittredge asked.

"We're gonna find out."

***

"Tyler, you got a backroom?" Clint asked.

"Uh, yeah . . ."

"Where?"

He pointed.

"Give me a hand."

Together they moved the three bodies into the backroom, where they would stay until it was all over.

"Williams," he called.

"Yeah?"

"Back room," Clint said

"With the bodies?"

"Would you rather be with the bodies," Clint said, "or be one of the bodies?"

Williams stepped into the room. As Clint started to close the door Williams asked, "Am I gonna live through this?"

"As long as I don't find out you were the one who shot the old man in the back. Or killed the girl."

Williams looked relieved. That's when Clint knew he was telling the truth about not being involved.

He closed the door and locked it.

When he came back into the saloon, he saw that the man who was a regular customer had finished eating, drank his beer, and put his head back on the table.

"Sorry about the window, Tyler," he said. "I assure you someone will pay to replace it. You can close up now, if you want."

"With bodies in my back room?"

"They'll be gone by morning," Clint said. "Guaranteed"

"Maybe I'll stay open," the bartender said. "You might need a drink when this is all done."

"I will," Festus said.

"That's fine," Clint said. "Then stay open."

Clint walked over and sat at a table with Festus, who was finishing a beer.

"Where are we goin' next?" the old man asked.

"Outside."

"Again?" Festus moaned. "On that deserted street?"

"That's where the action is going to be, Festus," Clint said. "You can pull out if you want. I appreciate what you've already done."

"No, no," Festus said, "I'm in til the end."

"Then have another whiskey and we'll get going," Clint told him.

Chapter Forty-Three

"Where are we goin'?" Festus asked, as they left the saloon. "We ain't gonna wander around the streets again, are we?"

"No," Clint said. "We're going to take up a position somewhere and wait. First, they have to find out where the shooting took place. Then they'll go from there."

"How many do you think?"

"According to Williams, two."

"And Noah Black?"

"He'll come later."

They walked across the street.

"Where will they be comin' from?" Festus asked.

"They're working for Kittredge," Clint said, "so they'll come from the South of Deadwood."

"Down the street."

"That's right."

"So where'll we wait?"

Clint stepped up onto the boardwalk across from the Last Stand.

"We're going to wait right here."

"How do we get 'em here?" Festus asked.

"I've got an idea," Clint said.

***

Beckett and Cartwright came out of the South of Deadwood Saloon and stopped.

"Which way?" Cartwright asked, looking left and right.

"We heard those shots," Beckett said. "Others must've, too, but there's nobody on the street."

"People are having their Thanksgivin'," Cartwright said, "but where's the sheriff?"

Beckett laughed.

"He must be hidin'," he said.

Suddenly they saw an old man running toward them. As he passed, Beckett yelled, "What's the rush?"

"A shootin' at the Last Stand," the old man answered. "I'm goin' for the sheriff! Ya'll better stay away from there." And he kept running.

Beckett looked at Cartwright and smiled.

"Let's go!"

***

Clint waited across the street from The Last Stand. He figured once Festus delivered his message, they would be along. Sure enough, two men came running from the direction of the South of Deadwood Saloon. Unwisely, they did not have their guns in their hands.

When they reached the street in front of The Last Stand they stopped. The smashed window made it obvious the action had taken place there.

They hesitated about going in, so Clint stepped out behind them.

"You boys looking for me?" he asked.

He noticed that at some point they had palmed their guns, so when they turned to face him, they were already firing. No time to try to talk them out of it.

Clint moved, throwing himself to the ground to his left, drawing his gun at the same time. As he came up to one knee, the two gunmen were already moving, looking for cover. There were horse troughs in front of the saloon, so they each ducked behind one.

Clint found cover behind a buckboard someone had left on the street, with one horse hitched to it. He had to hope the horse didn't get skittish and run off.

Clint had been in many gun battles over the years. As the two men continued to fire at him from cover, something happened that had never happened before, in all those years. As he rose up and started to fire back, the horse bolted and started running, taking his cover with it.

He tried to run along until he could find more cover, but the animal started moving too fast. In moments he was out in the open and fair game.

The two men rose up, thinking they had him at their mercy. As he pointed his gun at them and pulled the trigger, it happened. That thing that had never happened before, in all his years.

His gun jammed.

Unable to fire back, he actually was at the mercy of the two men. He was aware that Festus was running back up the street as fast as he could, but he was too far away to offer him any help.

"It's all over, Gunsmith," one of the men said. They both extended their guns for their final shots, laughing as they did so.

At that moment the batwing doors of The Last Stand swung out, and a man appeared, gun in hand. He fired several shots, striking both men in the back and dropping them where they stood. In moments it was quiet, and they were dead in the street.

Clint looked at his gun, which had betrayed him for the first time in his life. Now that the gun battle was over, he managed to clear the jam. He holstered it and walked toward the dead men.

The man who had come out of the saloon tucked his gun back into his belt.

"You saved my life," Clint said. "What's your name so I can thank you?"

"They call me Targett."

"I know that name," Clint said. "You used to have quite a rep."

"Not for a long time," the man said. "Those days are long gone."

"Well, I'm much obliged to you."

"Don't be," Targett said. "I shot them because they woke me up."

He turned and went back inside. That was when Clint realized he was the man who had his head down on the table for most of the day.

Festus came running up next to him and asked, "Who was that?"

"You wouldn't believe me."

Chapter Forty-Four

Art Kittredge and Noah Black listened to all the shooting, and then it stopped.

"What do you think?" Kittredge asked.

"Sounds promisin'," Black said.

"Well," Kittredge said, "go and find out."

"We'll find out soon enough," Black said.

***

Clint decided there was no need to go back into The Last Stand. His savior had probably returned to his table, and he deserved to be left alone.

"You sure that was him?" Festus asked.

"It was," Clint said, "but never mind." He looked up and down the street. There was still no sign of the onlookers a gunfight usually brought out. And there was also no sight of the sheriff.

"What now?" Festus asked. "Is it over?"

It was dusk and would soon be dark. Thanksgiving was coming to a close.

"No, it's not over," Clint said. "But it will be, soon."

"Then where do we go from here?"

"I think there's only one place *to* go," Clint said.

***

Kittredge and Noah Black had moved from the back room to Kittredge's office, where the saloon owner poured a couple of whiskies.

Black accepted the drink and said, "If it's over, you better get my money ready."

"Let's wait and see if it *is* over," Kittredge said. "Don't worry, you'll get paid."

There was one more thing Black had to do, but he didn't want to take it until he had his money. So he tossed down his whiskey and took his gun from his holster.

"I think you better pay me now, Kittredge," he said.

"All right, all right," Kittredge said, waving a hand. "Don't get all riled up. Your money's here." He opened a desk drawer. "See?"

"Put it on top of the desk," Black ordered.

"Now look—"

Black pointed the gun right at the man and said, "Now!"

"Okay, okay," Kittredge said. He was starting to believe that he was in trouble. He took the money promised to Noah Black and his boys and set it out on the desk. "There you go. Anything else?"

"No," Black said, "that's it. Thanks." He pulled the trigger. The impact of the bullet at close range drove Kittredge back against the wall. He bounced off and fell to the floor, on his face, dead.

Black holstered his gun and went through Kittredge's desk until he found an envelope big enough to carry all the bills. A good portion of it was his, and if any of his men were killed, there would be more.

Still unsure as to whether or not the Gunsmith was dead, he decided not to wait at the saloon any longer. He went out the back door.

**

Clint and Festus reached the South of Deadwood and Clint pounded his fist on the door. It was opened by the bartender.

"We're closed for Thanksgivin', Mr. Adams," he said.

"I don't care," Clint said. "I want to see Kittredge and anyone who's with him."

"Who d'ya think is with him?"

"A fella named Noah Black," Clint said. "Tell me I'm wrong or get out of the way."

"Yeah, Yeah, okay," the man said, backing away. "He was in the back room, but he might be in his office now. I heard a shot a while ago."

"A shot?" Clint said. "Did you go and see what it was."

"There've been a lot of shots tonight," the bartender said.

Clint looked at Festus.

"You check the back room, I'll check the office."

"Right."

Clint crossed the empty saloon floor and stopped at the door. Before going in, he once again checked his gun to be sure it wouldn't jam again. Keeping it in his hand, he opened the door and went in. It looked empty, but he could smell the gunshot in the air. He looked around, and when he checked behind the desk, he found Kittredge's body. He turned the man over, found he had been shot once. He'd either had a falling out with the gunman, Noah Black, or this was somebody's plan, all along.

Festus came in and said, "Back room's clear. What about here?"

"Kittredge is here," Clint said. "He's dead. Somebody shot him."

"I thought they were workin' for him."

"Apparently, they're working for somebody else."

"Who?"

"I can only think of one person."

Clint holstered his gun. They were about to leave when another man stepped into the room and pointed a gun at them.

"What the hell's goin' on?" Sheriff Haley asked.

Chapter Forty-Five

"Put the rifle down, Festus," Haley said.

Festus looked at Clint.

"What are you trying to pull, Haley?" Clint asked. "The shooting is all over, and you decide to come out of your office and play lawman?"

"I ain't playin', Adams," Haley said. "Where's Kittredge?"

"He's right there," Clint said, pointing.

Haley came around to look at the dead man.

"Did you kill 'im?"

"I didn't have to," Clint said. "I'm guessing Noah Black did."

"Who's he?"

"Don't play dumb, Haley," Clint said. "This is almost all over. Why don't you just go back to hiding in your office?"

"I want your gun, Adams," Haley said.

"We've gone through this already," Clint said. "If you want my gun, you're going to have to take it. Otherwise just get out of the way."

Clint wondered if the man was suddenly going to get brave and make him draw on a badge, which he didn't want to do.

Haley did a lot of thinking in a few seconds, then gritted his teeth and said, "Damn you, Adams!"

"Put the gun away," Clint said.

Haley holstered his gun.

"You can make yourself handy by having the bodies picked up from The Last Stand, and out here."

"Where are you gonna be?" Haley asked.

"I'm going to be looking for Noah Black," Clint said. "I have the feeling he's the back shooter, and he probably killed Millie."

"And who paid him and his men?"

"His men thought Kittredge was paying, but I'm having my doubts. If I can take Black alive, he should confirm my suspicions."

"Kathleen Sterling?"

"I think you know who I mean, Sheriff." He walked past the man. "Come on, Festus. Let's finish this."

Festus followed Clint out of the office, across the empty floor, and out the door.

***

Letty Miller and Kathleen Sterling had been spending their Thanksgiving busily pleasuring each other. After dinner they had gone right back to bed, doing everything two women could do to each other to make them happy. And Letty was paying so much attention to Kathleen that she wasn't wondering what was happening out on the street.

Now they were so feverishly eating each other's wet boxes that they almost didn't hear the pounding on the door.

"What was that?" Kathleen asked, breathlessly lifting her. Her face was shiny with Letty's juices.

Letty reluctantly did the same and said, "I think somebody's at the door."

Both women sat up and wiped their faces with the bed sheet.

"I better go and see who it is," Letty said. "It might be important."

"It might be the end we've been waiting for," Kathleen said, excitedly.

Letty stood and put on her robe.

"I'll go and see."

"Hurry back!" Kathleen said, sliding her hand down between her legs. "I'm far from done."

She began busily moving her fingers as Letty left the room, more convinced than ever that Sterling had found his young wife in a Denver whorehouse.

***

Noah Black continued to pound his fist on the door of Letty Miller's house. When she finally answered, her face was flushed, her hair was in disarray, and her big nipples were poking out under her robe.

"Sorry to interrupt you," he said, "but I thought you might like to know that Kittredge is dead."

"Did he pay you?"

"Oh, yes," Black said, lifting the envelope in his left hand.

"Then Clint Adams is dead?" the mayor asked.

"Well . . . maybe."

"Maybe?"

"I guess you couldn't hear all the shots from here," Black said. "Or you were too busy to notice."

"Come in," Letty said, folding her arms beneath her breasts and backing away.

Noah Black entered, and she closed the door. They walked into the living room.

"So who's upstairs?" he asked, with a smirk.

"Kathleen Sterling came over for Thanksgiving dinner," Letty said.

"And you two have been . . . busy?"

"Yes, we have," Letty said. "She's waiting upstairs to hear the news."

"And you want me to give it to her?"

"I want to know that Clint Adams is dead," she told him.

"And you're saving her for later?"

"Kittredge never should've paid you until we were sure Adams was dead."

"Well," Black said, "I really didn't give him much of a choice."

"If Clint is still alive, when will you take care of him?" she asked.

"If he's still alive it means all my men are dead," Black said.

"Then you'll have to take care of him yourself."

"If he's still alive and all my men are dead, I guess that means he's not as past it as I thought."

"What are you telling me?" she asked. "You're not going to face him?"

"Well . . . I did get paid, already."

"But you're not done."

"Do you mean Adams, or the Sterling, girl?"

"You can take care of her right now," Letty said.

"Really?" Black asked. "Are you done with her?"

"I almost was when you pounded on my door," Letty said, "but it's no never mind. You can do it now, and then we'll discuss Adams."

"Whatever you say, Miss Mayor."

Letty watched Noah Black go up the stairs, wishing the man had waited ten minutes more.

***

Noah Black went up the stairs and found Kathleen in Letty's bed, lying on her back with her hand busy between her legs. He watched for a few seconds, wishing he had time to help her, then approached the bed.

Kathleen had her eyes closed but sensed someone was there.

"I'm glad your ba—" she started, assuming it was Letty, but she stopped when she saw Noah Black. "What're you doin' here? Is it all over?"

"Almost," he said, and drew his gun.

"Wha—wait," Kathleen said. "What're you doin'?"

"My job."

"No!" Kathleen said, suddenly getting it. "Letty!" she shouted.

He pulled the trigger.

***

Downstairs, Letty heard the scream and then shot, and felt a little sad. But she recovered enough to walk to a breakfront against the wall and take a gun from the top drawer.

Noah Black came down, smiling.

"It looked to me like you ladies wasn't done," he said, as he reached the bottom of the stairs. "Could be I can help ya with that."

"That would be nice," Letty said, "if I had the time."

"Right, right," he said. "Adams. He's probably on the way over here. After all, he's gotta have it all figured out."

"Well," she said, "he thinks he's got it all figured out. So do you."

"What?"

He stopped as Letty brought the gun out from behind her back.

"Whatta you—" he said and went for his gun. Luckily, he wasn't fast enough, since she was already pulling the trigger—once, twice, and then again, just to be sure.

When Black was on the floor, she ran to the body, picked up the envelope full of money and rushed to put it in the drawer of the breakfront.

She turned as her front door crashed open and Clint Adams came rushing in.

Chapter Forty-Six

"I'm so glad you're here, Clint," Letty gushed. "This man was crazy!"

Clint walked to her and took the gun from her hand. She leaned forward, putting her head on his chest.

"It was horrible!" she cried. "He went upstairs, and . . . and . . ." She sobbed.

"Take a look upstairs, Festus."

"Right."

While the old man went upstairs, Clint took Letty over to the sofa and sat her down.

***

When Festus got upstairs, he froze in the doorway for a second. The girl on the bed was incredibly beautiful, even in death. He approached the bed to make sure and saw the bullet hole right between her breasts. He couldn't believe somebody had killed such a lovely creature.

He turned to go back downstairs.

***

When Festus came down he said to Clint, "There's a dead girl upstairs, in bed. She's, uh, naked."

Clint was standing by the sofa. He looked down at Letty, who took her hands from her face.

"H-he killed her!" she blurted.

"And you killed him," Clint said. "That's impressive."

She glared at him and pulled her robe tightly closed, as the slopes of her breasts had been showing.

"He was a horrible man, and he was going to . . . to . . . I told him I had money in the breakfront, and that was where I had the gun. I just kept . . . pulling the trigger."

"Festus, check the breakfront." He didn't want Letty to do it, in case she had another gun. He still didn't trust her, in spite of what this tableau depicted.

Festus went, opened the drawer, took the envelope out and looked inside.

He whistled and said, "It's full of money."

"Of course it is," Clint said.

He glared down at Letty, who looked a mess, but who—he was sure—had gotten everything her own way. He just couldn't prove it, because everybody was dead.

"I-I guess you'll have to tell the sheriff what I've done," she said.

Chapter Forty-Seven

By the morning after Thanksgiving, the bodies had been cleaned up and the undertaker was busy. Since Clint and Festus had gotten a beef jerky and beans Thanksgiving, Clint offered Festus a big breakfast that next morning. They met at the café where Slim, the waiter, showed them to a table. There were other diners there, as the streets of Belle Fourche were once again active. Everyone seemed to know that all the shooting was done.

Clint and Festus got long looks as they followed Slim. Apparently, word was out that they were the only two survivors of all the shooting.

When they were seated, Clint told Slim to bring them both steak-and-eggs.

"So what're you gonna do today?" Festus asked.

"Leave town, I guess," Clint said. "I've got friends living about three hours from here who invited me for Thanksgiving. They've got two kids, but maybe there'll be leftovers."

"What about the mayor?" Festus asked. "You still sure she was involved?"

"I can be as sure as I want to be," Clint said. "I can't prove a thing."

"So she's gonna get away with all of it?"

"Looks like it," Clint said.

"That don't seem right."

"It isn't," Clint said. "But what can I do about it?"

"Well," Festus said, "I guess I could keep my eye on her, but nobody's gonna give me any never mind."

"Forget about it, Festus," Clint said. "Just go back to doing whatever you were doing before I got you involved."

"Which is nothin'," Festus pointed out. "After all this I don't know if I can go back to that."

Slim brought their plates and both men dug in hungrily. They didn't speak again until they had both finished.

"That was damn good!" Festus praised. "Thanks."

"You deserve more than that," Clint said. "You probably saved my life."

"Not like that feller in the Last Stand did," Festus said. "You gonna thank him?"

"I think he just wants to be left alone," Clint said, "and I've got to say, I don't much blame him."

They left the café after Clint paid the bill.

"I guess I'll go on back to my hotel room," Festus said.

"And I'll go on to the livery and saddle my horse. You take care, Festus."

The two men shook hands.

"You watch yer back, Clint."

"I always do."

Festus walked back to his broken-down hotel. Clint headed for the livery.

***

Clint was saddling his Tobiano when Sheriff Haley walked up.

"I thought I'd find you here," Haley said.

"What's on your mind, Sheriff?"

"Everything," Haley said. "What you said to me last night, about staying in my office. A lot of people died last night."

"It wasn't my fault," Clint said, tightening the cinch.

"I never said it was," Haley said. "I think we both know who was responsible for it all."

"And we can't prove a damn thing," Clint said. "Not with everybody dead."

"You said you weren't leaving until you could prove who back shot Sterling,"

"I proved it to my satisfaction," Clint said.

"And are you going to accept that she gets away with it?"

"I'm going to have to," Clint said. "I've had enough of this town."

Clint walked the Tobiano out, with Haley trailing along.

"What do you want me to tell you, Sheriff?" Clint asked. "I can't help you justify your actions. Or your lack of action. You're going to have to live with that."

Clint mounted up and rode away from the livery, leaving Haley standing there with his thoughts.

***

But he couldn't just ride out. Not when he had to pass by City Hall to do it. So he reined his horse in, tied it off, and entered the hall. He went directly to the mayor's office and found her behind her desk.

"I suppose you're here to say goodbye," she said.

"I'd actually like to say more than that."

"Clint," she said, in a chiding tone, "are you still thinking badly of me? After what happened last night?"

"Especially after what happened yesterday."

"You mean to that poor, beautiful girl, Kathleen?" Letty asked.

"She was involved as much as you were, Letty," Clint said. "It's too bad she didn't see you coming."

"That man killed Kathleen."

"Yes, for you."

"You still insist on believing he worked for me?" she said "He worked for Kittredge. That man who survived, Williams, told you that."

"That's because Williams believed that."

She sat back in her chair and shook her head.

"It distresses me that you think so badly of me," she said. "I thought you and I had something that first night."

"I let you put one over on me, Letty, with sex," Clint said. "I'll have to live with that and be a little more careful who I sleep with."

"Come, come, Clint," she said. "You're a man. There's nothing you can do about that."

"No," he said, "it seems like there's nothing I can do about any of this. And that's going to stick in my craw for a long time to come."

"You're a dear man," she said, "and I'm going to remember that first night for a long time."

"And unfortunately," he said, "I am, too."

He turned, left City Hall, and rode out of Belle Fourche with a cold lump in his stomach.

Chapter Forty-Eight

It didn't seem to take long for him to ride to the Sturdivant ranch.

Clint had met Ivan "Bull" Sturdivant many years ago, before the man had become a successful rancher. He wasn't a rich man, but he had enough land and cattle to support his wife and two kids.

When Clint rode up to the ranch house, Sturdivant was leaning on his corral, talking with one of his ranch hands. When he saw Clint, he came rushing over and reached him as he dismounted.

"You made it!" he said, pumping Clint's hand, "I told Lisa you would." His grip was powerful, as he stood a good six-foot-five.

"I missed Thanksgiving," Clint said, "but I was hoping for some leftovers, Bull."

"There is plenty," his friend said. "Lisa said she was making enough for ten."

"I'm glad to hear it," Clint said. "I was upset that I had missed out."

"Andy!" Sturdivant yelled to his hand, who ran over. "Take Mr. Adams' horse to the barn and see to it."

"Yes, sir."

"Come to the house," Sturdivant said, putting his arm around Clint's shoulders as they walked. "Lisa and the kids will be excited to see you."

"How old are the kids now?" Clint asked. "They don't even know me."

"Eric is six and Mandy is four. I've told them all about you. So much, in fact, that they already call you 'Uncle Clint.' When is Uncle Clint coming, they ask."

Sturdivant opened the door and ushered Clint into the house. It sprawled on one level, but you could tell that the man had built it with his own hands.

"The house is beautiful," Clint said.

"I am going to add a second level," Sturdivant said. "We want to have more kids."

His friend had exactly the kind of life a Gunsmith would never have. On the other hand, Clint didn't really want this, but he was happy for his friend.

"Lisa! We have company!"

Lisa Sturdivant came rushing out to see what her husband was yelling about.

"Clint!" She rushed to him and took him into her arms. She was a small, pretty woman with surprising strength.

"I told you he would come," Sturdivant said.

"He is a liar," she told Clint. "*I* told him you would come, and I was going to cook plenty."

"He is anxious for leftovers," Sturdivant told his wife. "He missed Thanksgiving."

"We will have another Thanksgiving," she assured Clint, "and I'll feed you so much you'll burst."

"I'm looking forward to it."

"The children are in their room," she said. "I'll get them. They are anxious to meet Uncle Clint."

As she went to fetch them, Clint leaned over to Sturdivant and asked, "What do I have to do as Uncle Clint?"

"Just be yourself," Sturdivant told him.

"What've you told them?"

"That you are my longtime friend."

"Nothing about . . ."

"No, no," Sturdivant said, "no talk of reputations or guns."

"Good, good."

Lisa returned with two little imps. Though they were two years apart, they were the same size. The girl seemed to have her father's size, while the boy emulated his mother. They were fine looking children and, for a while, Clint forgot all about Belle Fourche.

Chapter Forty-Nine

True to her word Lisa Sturdivant laid out so much food, Clint thought he would burst. It was the finest Thanksgiving—or day after Thanksgiving—meal he had ever had.

After supper Clint went out on the front porch with Sturdivant, while Lisa and the children cleaned up.

"You're not leaving, are you, Uncle Clint?" Eric asked.

"No, no," Ivan Sturdivant said. "Clint is going to be stayin' with us for a while."

"Maybe a few days," Clint told Eric."

"Yay!" the little boy cheered and ran to tell his mother and sister.

On the porch Sturdivant produced two cigars, and, while they smoked, Clint told his friend about Belle Fourche.

"My God!" Sturdivant said, when Clint was finished. "You should have come and got me to back you."

"Not a chance," Clint said. "I wasn't about to take you away from your family for the holiday."

"Well, from what you tell me, I'm glad I never go to Belle Fourche."

"Where do you get your supplies? Deadwood?"

"No, I won't go there, either. Sturgis is closer and, although small, I can get everything I need there."

"It's just as well," Clint said. "There are no fond memories for me in either place."

"So you really think that lady mayor was behind everything that happened?"

"I do," Clint said. "When they told me that she was ruthless, they weren't kidding."

"It must eat at you that you had to leave without proving it."

"It does."

"I'm surprised you were able to tear yourself away."

"Well," Clint said, "I knew I was coming here for leftovers."

"And you're still only about three hours away."

"What are you saying?"

"Nothin'," Sturdivant replied. "Just that you're not too far away, if you should suddenly think of a way of proving she was behind everything."

"I can't prove it," Clint said, bitterly.

"But?"

"But what?"

Sturdivant shrugged.

"I just thought I heard a 'but'."

Clint walked to the edge of the porch and puffed on his cigar.

"You want a drink?" Sturdivant asked.

"Sure."

"Whiskey or lemonade?"

"I'll take a whiskey."

Sturdivant went into the house. Moments later the door opened. Clint turned and saw little Mandy standing there.

"Hi, sweetie."

"Why are you sad, Uncle Clint?"

"I'm not sad, honey."

"You look sad," she said. "Do you need a hug? Momma says sad people need hugs."

"I'd like a hug very much."

He put his cigar down on the rail and crouched down. Mandy came to him, put her arms around his neck and gave him a mighty hug. Then she stepped back and looked into his eyes.

"Is that better?"

"That is much better, Mandy. Thank you."

She turned and ran back into the house, past her father, who was coming out with two whiskies.

"What was that about?" Sturdivant asked, handing him a glass.

"She said I looked sad and needed a hug."

"Ah," he said, "that little girl's hugs are like magic. Did it work?"

"Yes." Clint sipped his whiskey.

"So you're going to forget about Belle Fourche?"

"I can't."

"You're going back there, aren't you?" Sturdivant asked.

"Yes."

"When?"

"A few days," Clint said. "I still need to give it some thought."

"You'll figure out a way to nail that lady mayor," Sturdivant told him.

"How do you know that?"

"Because I know you," his friend said. "You'll never be able to let this go."

"You knew that from the moment I told you the story, didn't you?"

"Oh yeah," Sturdivant said.

"Did you send your little girl out here to hug me?" Clint asked.

"No, I didn't," Sturdivant said. "But it worked, didn't it?"

"It sure did."

Chapter Fifty

Clint stayed for three days, talked with Sturdivant and Lisa, let her feed him, played with the kids, and finally had to go back to Belle Fourche.

"Are you sure you won't stay longer?" Lisa asked. "The kids love you."

"What about you?"

"I love you, too," she said. "If you stay, I'll leave Ivan and marry you."

"Hey," he said, "I may just take you up on that."

"No you won't," she laughed.

Sturdivant had Andy bring Clint's Tobiano around after breakfast. He kissed Lisa and the kids goodbye, then walked to his horse with Sturdivant.

"Come back when it's over," his friend said. "Your bed's always here."

"Thanks, Bull," Clint said, "but when I've finished what I have to do in Belle Fourche, you won't want me around. I'll have to hit the trail to clear my head."

The two men shook hands, and Clint mounted up and rode off.

Lisa came out and stood on the porch with her husband, watching Clint leave.

"You knew he'd go back, didn't you?" she asked. Her husband had told her the whole story.

"Didn't you?"

'Oh, yes," she said. "He couldn't just ride away and let that woman get away with everything she did. That's not something your friend could do."

"No, it's not," Sturdivant said.

"Do you think we'll ever see him again?" she asked.

"Sure," Sturdivant said. "We'll see him next Thanksgiving."

"I'll cook like he's coming," she said.

Ivan Sturdivant put his arm around his wife and held her close.

***

When Clint rode back into Belle Fourche, the street was busy. It looked like midday in any other town, like the events of the week before had never happened. People didn't even stare as he rode in.

He decided to go to that broken down hotel on a side street and get himself a room. He didn't really want anyone to know he was there.

When he asked the desk clerk for a room, the man said, "Are you sure?"

"Give me one across from Festus."

The man shrugged and said, "Take any one you want. They ain't locked."

"Is there a livery near here?"

"End of the street," the man said, "but it's just as broken down as this place."

"Is the hostler any good?"

"He's as good at his job as I am at mine," the man said.

Clint decided to try it anyway.

He took his horse to the livery and woke the hostler up.

"I'll rub him down and feed him myself," he said.

"I kin do it," the older man said. "I like horses a lot better than people."

"I know how you feel," Clint said, deciding to trust the man.

He went back to the hotel, and up to the second floor. The room across from Festus' was small and dusty, but he figured all he had to do was take the blanket off the bed and shake it out. It'd be fine.

He went across the hall and knocked. He had to do it several times before he heard footsteps, and the door opened.

"Well, it's about time," Festus said.

"You were expecting me?"

"I figured you'd be back," Festus said. "Come on in."

Clint entered and Festus closed the door, Gracie was leaning in a corner.

Festus walked to his bed and sat down.

"So what're we doin'?"

"I don't think I'll need my back watched," Clint said, "unless she's got herself some new gunmen already."

"She's been actin' like a real mayor, for a change," Festus said. "But I don't expect that to last."

"What's going on with the South of Deadwood?"

"That bartender's runnin' it," Festus said. "Doin' a good job, too."

"And the Last Stand?"

"Closed down," Festus said. "Never did get that window replaced."

"I thought you said she was acting like a real mayor," Clint reminded him.

"Not that good a mayor. You know, it's probably good you came back now."

"Why?"

"There's a meetin' of the Town Council tomorrow mornin'," Festus said.

"You don't say."

"Might be just the thing for you."

"How about breakfast tomorrow?" Clint asked. "No point in me attending that meeting on an empty stomach."

Chapter Fifty-One

Slim was glad to see Clint back and served him and Festus a feast of a breakfast. When they were done, they left and stopped out front.

"City Hall?" Festus asked.

"I think the sheriff's office first."

"Whataya think he's gonna do?"

"I'm going to give him a chance to do something, for a change."

They walked to the sheriff's office and entered. Haley looked at him in surprise.

"What the—I thought you left town."

"I did," Clint said, "but I had to come back. I wanted to give myself and you a chance to make things right."

"How do we do that?" Haley asked.

"First, can you think of anyone who could replace Letty as mayor?"

Haley thought a minute, then said, "Two. They're on the Council."

"Okay," Clint said, "and second, are you willing to be a real sheriff?"

Haley sat back in his chair.

"I been thinking about that since you left."

"I hear there's a Town Council meeting this morning," Clint said. "I thought I'd attend."

"You want company?"

"I thought you'd never ask."

***

"I'll just wait out here for ya," Festus said, "me and Gracie."

"I don't expect any shooting," Clint said, "but I'm glad you're here."

He went inside, looked into the mayor's office and found it empty. There were several other rooms, but Haley pointed him to the right one.

"I'll stay out here until I'm needed," the lawman said.

"And you'll back my play?"

"To the hilt," Haley promised.

Letty Miller was standing at the head of a long table, where five men were seated. They all looked at him as he entered.

"Clint!" Letty said. "I thought you left town."

"I had to come back," he replied. "Unfinished business."

"Is that right?" she asked. "Do you want to talk about it in my office?"

"No, right here'll be fine," he said.

"I don't think these fine gentlemen—"

"I think these gentlemen would like to hear how their mayor planned the bloodiest Thanksgiving in history, just to get her way."

"Clint, please," Letty said, as the five men stirred. They had seemed very bored when Clint first entered. Now their interest was up.

"Starting with working with Kathleen Sterling to kill her husband, and ending with you having Kathleen killed in your own bed, and then killing your hired gunman yourself so you wouldn't have to pay anyone. Of course, that was after you couldn't kill me and pin the blame on me."

The five men looked around at each other, then stared at Letty.

"Not to mention working with Art Kittredge, until you didn't need him anymore and had him killed."

"Clint!" she snapped. "These gents won't ever believe I'd do anything like that."

"I'd believe it," one man said, "I just thought nobody would ever have the nerve to say it."

Clint thought this must be one of the men the sheriff said could be mayor.

"Mayor Miller's had this town under her thumb for a long time," Clint said. "Including all you gents in this room. Now I'm not sure why she was able to do that, except that she had the will, and you boys let her."

"Nobody ever accused her of anything," another man said.

"Did she really have Walt Sterling killed?" a third man asked. "He was a fine old gent."

"We all liked Walt," another man said. "We thought he was gonna run again."

"He never would have beat me," Letty said.

"Oh, I think he might've," the first man said.

"She couldn't take that chance," Clint said, "so she hired a gunman to shoot him in the back, and thought she could blame me, simply because I was in town."

The men started talking to each other and ignoring Letty.

"He can't prove any of this," she said.

Now they looked at her, and then Clint.

"Can you?" the first man asked.

"I don't have to," he said. "I just need you five to believe it."

The first man looked at the others and said, "I believe it."

"So do I," another man said.

"You can't be serious."

"I'll tell you who else believes it," Clint said. "Sheriff Haley."

"That idiot?"

"She kept him out of the way while she put her plan into action," Clint said. "Sheriff!" he called.

Haley came into the room.

"Miss Mayor," Haley said, "I think I'm gonna put you under arrest and let a court of law figure it all out."

"You've got no witnesses!" she snapped.

"I think I'd be a pretty good witness, myself," Haley said. He walked over to Letty and took hold of her arm. "Let's walk over to the jail."

As he walked the mayor from the room Clint asked, "Which one of you is named Faracy."

"That'd be me," said the first man who had spoken.

"Sheriff Haley tells me you'd be a good replacement for the mayor."

"I think so, too."

"What do the rest of you think?"

They were all for it. Faracy stood and went to the head of the table.

"Gentlemen," Clint said, and walked out.

***

On the street Festus said to Clint, "I saw the sheriff walk the mayor out. She was mad as a wet cat. Is it over?"

"It's over for me," Clint said. "The rest is going to be up to the town. If they play it right, they can get a new start."

"So you leavin'?"

"I'm leaving, Festus," Clint said. "I'm walking right to the livery and getting out of this town—for good!

Upcoming New Release

J.R. ROBERTS

THE GUNSMITH

40TH ANNIVERSARY EDITION

THE FRIENDLY GOLD MINE
BOOK 480

Clint Adams comes to Denver at the invitation of his friend, Talbot Roper. The best private detective in the country is about to embark on a new venture. He owns part of a new gold mine in Nelson, Nevada. He wants Clint not only to be his partner, but to look the mine over and advise him on whether or not it's a good investment. When they arrive, they discover that others are also interested in the mine. While they are investigating the mine's potential, they are also fighting to keep it. In this 40th anniversary edition of the Gunsmith series, will Clint Adams strike it rich?

**For more information
visit:** www.SpeakingVolumes.us

On Sale Now!

A Special Christmas Edition

THE JINGLE BELL TRAIL

For more information
visit: <u>www.SpeakingVolumes.us</u>

On Sale Now!

THE GUNSMITH GIANT SERIES

On Sale Now!

THE GUNSMITH *series*
Books 430 – 479

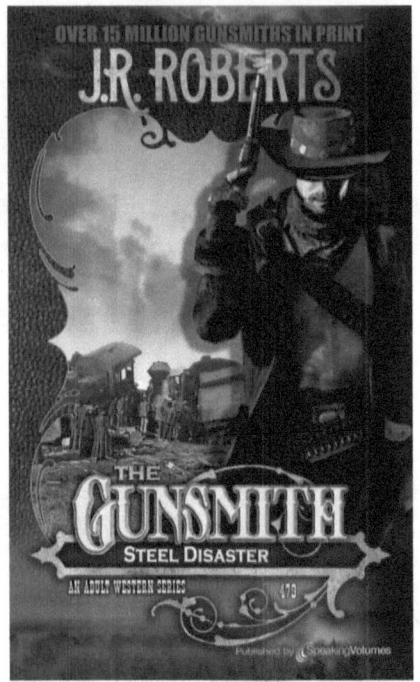

For more information
visit:

On Sale Now!

LADY GUNSMITH
BOOKS 1 - 10

**For more information
visit:** www.SpeakingVolumes.us

Sign up for free and bargain books

Join the Speaking Volumes mailing list

Text

ILOVEBOOKS

to 22828 to get started.

Message and data rates may apply.

www.ingramcontent.com/pod-product-compliance
Lightning Source LLC
Chambersburg PA
CBHW050512260626
47157CB00004B/1287